Freaky Tales

By

Sabrina B. Scales

Copyright 2019 Sabrina B. Scales

All rights reserved.

Cover Art: tverdohlib/Adobe Stock

Dedication

To every woman bold enough

to embrace the freedom of sexuality,

these stories are for you.

Be not afraid to,

Do whatever the fuck you wanna do.

Wherever the fuck you wanna do it.

Whenever the fuck you wanna do it.

With whomever the fuck you wanna do it with.

Because you fucking can…

Synopsis

Melody's Truth

Fantasies? I live those.

Orgasms? Yeah, I give those.

Fairytales? Never wanted to live those

Because I'm simply not that chick

Hearts? Yeah, I broke some

Love? These niggas can't get none

Commitment? I'm probably the wrong one

But you can stop by and lick this clit

If a freak is what you're looking for

Be prepared when you step through my door

On the bed, couch, or kitchen floor

I can give you what you need

I prefer my kisses down low

We can do this fast or we can go slow

Either way, I think it's best I let you know

When it's over, please, get up and leave

My name is Melody Bledsoe and I got some freaky things to tell you.

Are you ready?

Probably not!

Tale I
Ménage à Trois

I

Melody

Although I didn't necessarily date, I'd been *with* Maurice for two years. We shared living quarters and designated body parts on a regular basis, and even ate from the same pot of spaghetti when I was in a good mood. His sister, a good friend of mine, had introduced us in hopes of changing the strange fruit she'd considered me to be, based solely on the fact that I was a black woman who owned a cat, and she'd never seen me in public on the arm of a man. Unfortunately for her, I wasn't at a point in my life where traditional relationship goals were desirable. And instead of falling in love, getting married, and filling our apartment up with babies, the premise of me and Maurice's relationship was sex. Blissful, loud, ElephantTube-worthy sex.

There were two bedrooms in our tiny abode, and when I didn't wanna be fucked, eaten alive or bent over the dresser, I'd retire to my room and he'd retire to his. No feelings were allowed unless they led to orgasms, and if other shit came up, I would simply shut down. Contrary to his sister's belief that he was a regular, degular, shmegular nigga, Maurice had more kinks about him than an African braiding shop.

And I loved that shit.

We were never short on new and exciting things to do in the sack. And seeing as I bored easily, that worked to his and my advantage.

Every once in a while, he'd suggest something spicy and I'd usually go along. Didn't even flinch when he asked if I'd peg him, although I questioned his sexuality from that night on. I mean seriously, what straight man wants to be fucked in the ass with a dildo, or anything for that matter? None that I'd ever met. That's for damned sure.

In any event, I did it because it turned him on. And it didn't hurt that he bought a double-headed dildo, so I could fuck myself while I was fucking him. Whatever warm tingly lube he'd used made the experience fun for the both of us. And I wanted to do it more often than I cared to admit because for some reason, seeing a man in such a vulnerable state, having his body invaded in such an intimate way, made me feel dominant. Dangerously so.

"So, you got plans for tonight?" Maurice asked one Saturday night, blowing out a deep breath as he tiptoed past my crazy cat, Tuna, in route from the kitchen to the living room after cleaning our dinner plates.

"Nope. Sleep and more sleep. Why?" I turned my head to the side to find him grinning, fingers folded in his lap on top of a pair of black joggers.

"I was thinking maybe we could… do that thing I was asking you about." His thick legs spread, no doubt making room for an impending erection.

Since treating a woman like an object without a name was the basis of nearly every porn video I'd ever watched, I don't know why Maurice was having such a hard time saying that he finally wanted to bring his friend over so they could share my pussy. It wasn't like I'd flat out told him no or given him any indication that I wasn't down. His boy, Delvin, was fine as fuck. Tall and caramel with heavy ass feet. If Maurice was cool with him fucking me in front of his face, who was I to pass on some potentially great dick?

"I already told you, just say when." I sighed, pulling a hand from my full belly and tucking it under a head full of pinned and wrapped hair as Tuna left her designated spot under the kitchen window to climb up on my lap.

"So, tonight's good?" He squinted, honey-brown eyes almost the exact color of his skin, glancing down at Tuna because she was bound to pounce on him at any minute.

"Duh!" I replied, bucking my eyes and petting the fat Tabby occupying most of my lap.

"Cool." He shook his head, picking his cellphone up off the coffee table and shooting Delvin a text.

"And one more thing." He looked up from his phone. "Could you maybe, like, do some yoga or hit the treadmill for a few minutes? D likes sweaty pussy."

"Wait, *what*?" I craned my neck, looking upside his head like he'd lost his damn mind. And I swear to sourdough bread, Tuna tilted her head too, staring at Maurice the same way I was.

He didn't say anything, just shrugged his shoulders and got up off the couch, all five feet and ten inches of him heading to the bedroom to freshen up.

"He'll be here in thirty minutes!" He yelled down the hall as Tuna stretched out on my lap.

I picked her fat butt up and draped her over my shoulder like a baby as I got up off the sofa and headed into my room. Yoga wouldn't produce enough sweat in that short amount of time, so I hit the treadmill to wake up the sweat glands for this sexy ass weirdo.

&

The crotch of my boy shorts were damp with sweat after running on the treadmill for fifteen minutes straight. With Tuna at the foot of my bed, slipping in and out of cat naps, I focused on her whiskers instead of the task at hand. Maurice peeped in like a creeper and watched me from the hallway, tracing his tongue across his lips, gripping his dick and walking away at the sound of the doorbell ringing. Neglecting to grab a towel because I didn't wanna pat any sweat away, I pulled my bedroom door closed behind me so that Tuna wouldn't wander out.

With my heart beating like thunder in my chest, I followed Maurice into the living room to take a seat on the sofa. He pulled the front door open and grinned as Delvin walked in, filling the space with illegal amounts of sexiness and the smell of his woodsy cologne.

"Wassup, Mel?" His smooth voice swam from the door to the living room after he and Maurice wrapped up their signature dap and hug. He headed in my direction and plopped down on the couch beside me after Maurice took a brown paper bag from his hand and placed it in the refrigerator.

"Hey." I glanced over at him, the faint scent of fabric softener on his white T-shirt forcing me to linger for a minute. "How do you always manage to smell so good?" I asked with a smidgeon of a smile on my otherwise stoic face, taking in the statuesque man who'd piqued my curiosity the first time he came over and whooped my ass in a game of UNO.

Delvin shrugged his broad shoulders. Even sitting, he appeared much larger than Maurice. Standing about four inches taller than him, it somehow made sense for Maurice to choose him to take on this particular task. I relaxed against the sofa as Maurice came in and took a seat to my left with Delvin comfortably settled in on my right, undressing me with his eyes. My pussy pulsated at the thought of what was about to take place. Chills traveled up my arms and legs, leaving fine hairs standing on end as I quickly leaned forward to uncork a bottle of Patron and poured myself two overflowing shots. Knocking them back one after another, I felt my blood warming in response to the smooth intoxicating liquid flowing down my throat. I shimmied my shoulders to pack down my thoughts because one couldn't go into this situation too heady. My chocolate legs were exposed all the way up to the top of my thighs, shorts doubling as underwear that weren't fit to step outside in. A thin white tank top covered my upper body, with no bra to mask the painful hardening of my nipples. I was visibly overly stimulated with two grown men flanking my body. Horny was an understatement. Me *and* these niggas were starving.

A series of the nastiest songs that R&B had to offer played from Maurice's Bluetooth speaker mounted on the wall above the TV. The air conditioner was set on North Pole, as usual, forcing my nipples to press against the inside of my top, nearly hard enough to poke holes through it. I didn't expect much conversation since we all knew what was up. And the proverbial stopwatch to the evening's events was set when Maurice planted an anxious hand on my thigh.

Rubbing up and down my sensitive skin, filling my belly with anticipatory butterflies, he tipped his chin, signaling for Delvin to join in, light eyes lidded with seduction. And Delvin didn't hesitate, caressing the opposite thigh, palm warm and soft as if he'd never used it for anything else. And he probably hadn't, seeing as he and Maurice worked together as seasoned customer service reps at a local cable company where a strenuous day of work included answering the fuck out of some phone calls. I chewed at the inside of my lip as each man's hand traveled to the tenderness on the insides of my thighs until they were both pulling my legs apart, opening the door to my musty pussy.

"Damn." Delvin's round eyes traveled straight between my legs. He pulled his bottom lip between his teeth at the sight of the wet spot in the crotch of my lavender shorts.

"You worked out in these?" He seemed strangely intrigued, sliding a long finger down my barely covered split, then pulling his finger to his nose to carry out his funky fetish.

"Yeah." I pretended to understand this shit, too turned on to give a damn why this nigga liked sweaty pussy.

"How long?" He asked, sliding forward on the sofa, fondling my pussy and staring at it like it was a fourth person in the room.

"Twenty minutes." I exaggerated, legs open so wide I might as well have been doing the splits. "I just got off the treadmill before you walked through the door."

I slid back against the sofa as they held my legs open, thigh muscles tight and straining against their hold.

"Oh yeah?" Delvin almost moaned, dick rising under a pair of red joggers that probably came from the same *freaky nigga* store that Maurice got his from.

"I bet that pussy tastes salty as fuck." He trailed his eyes up from between my legs and squinted at me. And in the back of my mind, I kept thinking that it was a damn shame to be so sexy and so strange.

But my thoughts were quickly interrupted when Delvin pulled the crotch of my shorts to the side, staring deeply into my eyes as he stirred a finger inside me. I let my head fall back against the sofa, peeping Maurice tugging at his dick and breathing erratically, so focused on Delvin fingering my pussy that it looked like he wanted to cry.

I squirmed in my seat, so wet I could drown a fish. "You like that shit?" Maurice spoke just above a whisper.

"You like lettin' my boy play with that pussy while I watch?" He was pulling at his dick so hard that I thought he might rip it through his pants.

"Ye... *yeah.*" I moaned, voice shaky from Delvin's digits digging inward and upward, applying pressure with precision as I invited him all the way in.

"How does it feel?" Maurice groaned out. *"Tell me!"* He begged with his mouth and eyes.

"Good." I rolled my hips against the palm of Delvin's hand, ignoring the pain of his and Maurice's nails digging into the inside of my thighs as they held my legs open wide.

"Shit!" I screamed, insides bubbling with heated urgency.

"I'm gonna cum!" My voice cracked, turned on by the sight of my titties bouncing beneath my tank top as Delvin's thrust rocked my frame.

He kept on fingering me, breathing hard and staring at me, daring me to close my eyes as he closed in on me. His lips were so close that I thought he might kiss me. But he didn't, thank God. Just stayed there, sweeping a minty breeze over my nose that was more intoxicating than the two shots I'd already taken.

Naturally, I tried to pull my legs closed, feeling the threat of climax nearing and wanting to hold it to myself. But Delvin wouldn't let me. Neither of them would. Pumping his fingers into my pussy faster and harder and so damn deep, until I finally reached my peak and squirted up the spread of his forearm.

"Fuck! That was beautiful!" Maurice's eyes went wide, hand still gripping his dick because he still hadn't busted a nut.

I saw stars and felt dizzy. But I didn't have time to recover before Delvin was up and, on his feet, ready for the next stage of this freaky excursion.

"Come on." He reached out a hand to me. I looked over at Maurice who quickly stood from the sofa too.

The three of us filed down the hallway and headed into Maurice's bedroom, which was bigger than mine, so it only made sense. I stood beside the bed like a life-sized doll as the two of them took it upon themselves to undress me without needing my permission. I held my arms in the air as they pulled my top off over my head, watching my nipples react to being exposed to the cool air whirling down from the ceiling fan. Wet noises sounded from my slick pussy lips when I opened my legs to let them take off my shorts. Delvin bent down then sniffed and licked my clit before he picked me up and put me in the bed, instructing me to sit my back against the handmade, cherry wood headboard as he and Maurice took off all their clothes.

I wouldn't say Maurice had a terrible body, but it paled in comparison to Delvin's. Where Maurice was naturally thick because rock-solid bodies ran in his family, Delvin's defined muscles were the result of working out six days a week. I'd be lying if I said I didn't drool looking at that shit. Two grown men hungrily disrobing before me, in such a rush to wreak havoc on my body, they could barely slide out of their socks. Though their body types were different, neither of them were lacking between the legs. Smooth, thick and long accurately described Maurice's dick, while long, thick and crooked at the tip was a better fit for his friend's. In any event, I was ecstatic. Finding one good dick was pure luck on most days but having two at my disposal in one night was as common as riding a unicorn to the pot of gold at the end of the rainbow.

I kept myself busy, fingering my pussy while they slipped on condoms, climbing into the bed one by one after deciding the order of things. My mouth watered at the thought of sucking Maurice's dick because it fit my mouth perfectly, offering a little bit of a stretch. And apparently, they'd read my mind because Maurice stood on the bed, placing his dick right in front of my face while Delvin took the southern route and planted his head between my legs.

With little to no warning, Delvin pushed my knees apart, sinking one then two fingers inside me, followed by slow lapping from his tongue. Unable to moan because Maurice had slid in between my lips, I rolled my pussy against Delvin's face, allowing the warmth from his tongue to bathe me.

"You taste so fucking good." Delvin's voice was muffled between my legs. A hum of gratitude from my lips sent rippled vibrations around the perimeter of Maurice's dick. And I choked as he shoved to the back of my throat, regurgitated Patron burning my esophagus.

Delvin spread my legs wider, pushing my knees up and leaving me completely open, darting his tongue in and out of me, slurping the wetness down my split. Then he latched onto my clitoris and sucked it until it hurt, blatantly disregarding the tortured convulsions sending me arching against his mouth. Saliva curdled on the bed of my tongue before spilling from my open mouth and dripping down my chin. I strained my eyes open and up on Maurice as he braced his hands on the back of my head and drilled into my face, ignoring the tears trailing down my cheeks. Desperately, he sucked his teeth, knees bending as he swelled, filling my mouth with the heaviness of his throbbing muscle, snaking down the length of my tongue and slowly sliding back out.

"You're fuckin' nasty." He stared down at me, face grimaced. "Letting me fuck your mouth while this nigga eats your pussy. You're a slut, Melody. Say it." He slid in then back out of my mouth, giving me three seconds to speak.

"I'm a slut." I lisped before he was back in my mouth, fucking it even harder this time.

"You fuckin' right." He smashed into my face, holding it there, dick reaching the back of my throat while I choked on it, unable to breathe until he finally pulled back and I coughed.

Intensity whirled in my belly as Delvin pushed my legs up farther and darted his tongue in my ass, wetting it just enough to dig his thumb in it and rotate. He popped Maurice on the leg, and without a single word exchanged, Maurice stood up in my mouth, plummeting deep deep down my throat one more time, then backed away and sat down beside me as Delvin anchored his arms around my hips and dragged my body down the bed until I was lying on my back.

"You ever been fucked in the ass, Mel?" Delvin asked, eyes hopeful.

"Yeah," I answered honestly. There wasn't much me and Maurice hadn't done.

In lightning speed, Maurice reached into the nightstand and grabbed that magical lube we'd used during his pegging session and handed it to Delvin. Delvin pushed my thighs apart until all of my business was on display, squeezing a dime-sized amount of lube on his fingertip and sliding his thumb back into my ass. I tightened around his digit, eyes falling closed in response to the familiar sensation of pain and anticipation. Maurice's dick stood erect in the curl of his palm as he watched Delvin finger me, tugging his lip between his teeth.

Delvin found the perfect stretch after rubbing his thumb in circles inside me and deciding that my ass was open wide enough to push his big dick in. I cringed, knowing the initial penetration was painful no matter how many times I'd done it. And as he gripped my thighs, pulling me down between his open legs and roping mine around his waist, I braced my palms on either side of me and waited for him to enter.

"Ah!" I screamed as his head pressed against the tight skin of my anus, finding Maurice's hand there to squeeze as Delvin pushed harder until he popped in.

He plunged in and stayed still, painfully stretching the walls of my asshole, begging me to open my eyes as he started to stroke me slowly.

"Is it too big?" He asked. But from the look in his eyes, he didn't plan on stopping either way. "Is this too much dick for you, Melody?" He whispered, licking his juicy lips as he looked down between his legs, taking in the perfect view of his manhood expanding in my ass.

I contemplated saying no. But then I thought, what could a man possibly gain from a woman telling him that he didn't have enough dick?

Nothing.

Absolutely nothing.

And aside from that, it'd be a god damn lie.

"Yeah." I whimpered. And it was the whole truth. It was way too much dick and the sweat beading on my forehead should've been all the validation he needed.

"Can you take it?" He sucked his teeth, squeezing all of his flesh inside my tight ass while Maurice released my hand to massage my titties and stroke his own dick.

I nodded my head *yes*, pussy throbbing and empty as the perimeter of my asshole felt like it was on fire. Maurice rose up on his knees, throwing one leg across my chest, sliding up until he was straddling my face. And then he parted my mouth with the tip of his dick and slowly sank through the barrier of my wet lips.

My mouth and ass were full of flesh, pussy creaming and begging to be filled up too. I trailed my fingers down the center of my belly, heat from inside me leading the way to the sensitive peak of my swollen nub. And I rubbed there, sending tingles and chills up my spine, as Delvin pressed his hands against the insides of my thighs, fucking me harder with sweat beading on his chest.

"Your ass is so tight." I could hear Delvin's voice though Maurice's body was a barrier as he continued to fuck my face.

"Bet that pussy tight too." He groaned, sliding one hand up my thigh and dipping his finger inside my pussy.

"Is the pussy tight, Reece?" Delvin asked, so deep in my ass it was a god damn shame.

"Hell yeah, it's tight," Maurice replied, dick surrounded by spit and suction from my lips.

"Come get some," Delvin instructed, and Maurice slid out of my mouth, allowing Delvin the freedom he needed to spin me around until my back was on his chest and I was in position to receive Maurice, making me the meat in a big-dick-nigga sandwich.

Maurice mounted me, resting his weight on top of my body with Delvin still beneath me, buried deep inside my asshole. Maurice plunged into my pussy, offering a fullness that made me dizzy. My ass and pussy were filled to capacity, and I didn't know whether to scream or lie there and explode.

"Shit!" I screamed out, so completely filled up that I could feel my pelvis expand. "Fuck my pussy and my ass, you nasty motha fuckas!"

My ass kissed the front of Delvin's thighs, slick with sweat and heavily compressed. My nipples made indentions in the firmness of Maurice's chest as he leaned in to kiss me, apparently out of his fucking mind. I would do anything with him in the bedroom, hence the dicks in all my holes. But kissing was a no-no, reserved for a nigga I'd never met. I turned my head to the side, giving him my neck, pussy slippery and wet around him while my asshole stretched for Delvin.

They were ravishing my body, showing no restraint.

Pounding me hard.

Stroking me deep.

Calling me a slut.

Smacking my ass until my skin burned with sensation. And pulling my hair until my neck was sore.

And I didn't give a damn as long as I came.

Wet, warm and throbbing, my behind smashed against Delvin's solid thighs. Having relinquished all control, I let my legs fall apart and enjoyed the tortuous harmony of this ride. Maneuvering my hips as much as I could, I found a rhythm between their bodies and rode the wave. My pussy quivered and purred, lips spread, bulb rubbing against the length of Maurice's shaft. I squeezed tighter around Delvin as he plunged deeper and deeper, drilling my asshole, showing complete disregard for any pain I might be in.

"I'm 'bout to cum." Delvin's voice vibrated against the back of my neck. "I'mma cum in your fuckin' ass. God damn, Melody!" He shouted, spit droplets flying from his lips and landing on the side of my face.

His thighs tensed against my behind, thrusts became faster and harder and less calculated. I felt him swelling, forcing my sphincter to open wider. A sharp pain circled in my ass as he pulled me down hard against him by my hips.

"Oh, *ooh!*" His voice shivered as he emptied inside of me, slapping my thighs and sucking the skin on the back of my neck while Maurice kept on stroking.

I'd already came once, sending my juices running down between my legs and onto Delvin lying under me. And another orgasm ripped through my pelvis as Maurice began to fuck me with an urgency.

"Fuck!" His head shot up, the warmth of his seeds shooting free inside me rendering him helpless to the climax that had taken him over.

"God damn, Mel!" His eyes were down and on me before they swept up to Delvin who was spent and fucking useless.

Tale II
One Night Stand

I

Melody

He was a friend of a friend and a fine one at that. Had money, drove a nice ride and stayed on a side of town where nobody knew my name. I didn't typically go for his type—clean cut with no warrants out for his arrest. But he'd do for the night. It wasn't like I was tryna bring him home to meet my mama.

Mike was his name, and the name I'd given him was a fake one to match the phone number I'd scribbled on a napkin and dropped in the pocket of his slacks when we brushed shoulders in the hallway at my home girl's boutique launch party. He was there with somebody, so I kept it discrete. But he and I both knew what would be going down as soon as he got a minute away from his girlfriend. There was no mistaking that *"I wanna taste yo' pussy"* look on his face every time our eyes met from across the crowded room. It was a shame that his girl couldn't see it. So preoccupied with making purchases that she had no idea her man was out here choosing.

"What the hell are you grinnin' at?" My friend and owner of the newest, hottest spot in Southeast Houston, Kendra, snuck up behind me, peeping over my shoulder almost catching me sending a racy text to Mike in response to the one he'd sent to me less than five minutes after I gave him my number.

Thirsty ass…

"What? I was *not* grinnin'." I yelled over the music, killing the screen and dropping the prepaid phone in my clutch. She knew Mike and his girlfriend and wouldn't be ok with me potentially breaking up their "happy" home.

"I saw you drop that foodstamp phone in your purse, bitch. You better not be in here with your bullshit tonight." She loudly warned, a smirk curling her thin lips as she stepped up beside me.

Though her idea of *bullshit* was my idea of a *good time*, I respected her enough to keep the truth to myself. "I'm not." I lied, bumping my curvy hip against her slender one. "I'm just here to support my friend. Ain't none of these bougie niggas my type, anyway."

"Oh, you mean *taken*?" She squeaked. "Cause I could've sworn that was your favorite."

"I've changed." My voice went up an octave, accepting a drink from the server who'd been on his feet all night keeping the bubbly flowing.

"Bitch, you ain't changed nothin' but your panties." She giggled. "And you probably ain't even wearin' none." With catlike eyes, she looked me up and down, stopping to join me as I busted out laughing.

"Ain't!" I wiggled my behind, catching Mike trying not to stare a hole through my maxi-dress from the corner of his eye.

I couldn't wait to see if the heaviness in his steps had anything to do with his package. It was my experience that niggas who walked with purpose did so for a reason; namely to destroy every pussy in their path.

"Triflin'." Kendra shook her head, taking a sip from her champagne flute. "What you gettin' into after this? You and Maurice got any plans?"

"Maurice is busy." I cut her off at the mention of her brother's name. "We have one thing in common and he's behind on his payments."

"Really, Mel?" She squinted as I kept my eyes forward, having found a way to look at Mike without anybody knowing. "You're a special kinda silly for filing pet support on my brother. He don't even like the damn cat."

"Like it or not, he knew coming into this that he'd be getting two pussies, not one." I rolled my eyes from Mike to Kendra's skinny ass. "And Tuna likes him. She told me herself."

I kept a straight face though my friend thought my cat's attachment to her brother was a figment of my imagination, seeing as she'd attacked him every time he walked through our apartment door. I also neglected to mention that her brother and I weren't really on speaking terms, because apparently, an entire two months after the threesome between me, him and Delvin, he was still feeling some type of way about me fucking him and his friend, even though it was his idea in the first place.

Maurice hadn't come home to do more than pack an overnight bag for the last couple of days. And I didn't give him any lip about it because, in all honesty, I understood. The freaky shit was all fun and games when he had me to himself, but the minute another nigga benefitted from this five-star pussy, it was a problem and he couldn't take it. Delvin had been texting me to let me know Maurice was crashing at his place to clear his head about the whole thing. He also dropped not so subtle hints about wanting me to sit on his face and let him squeeze his dick in my ass one more time. I politely turned him down because even *I* had limits. But I'll be damned if the thought of that tongue between my legs for thirty minutes didn't make my pussy cream.

"Tuna is a crazy bitch and so are you." Kendra's bony shoulders bounced with laughter. "I'mma go make my final round before we wrap things up. You good?" She asked on a deep breath.

"I'm great," I replied, slowly pulling my temp-cell from my purse. "And congratulations, again. I can't wait to show out in that Kendra Sway romper."

"Thank you, sweets." She leaned in to kiss my cheek. "And you better tag me on your raggedy-ass Insta Story!" She spun away on a pair of fuchsia heels that added just the right amount of flavor to her lemon-yellow wrap skirt and ice white camisole under a high collared denim blazer. Kendra could pull off any ensemble with that flawless golden skin. But those vibrant colors had my girl shining bright like a diamond.

As soon as she walked away, I opened the text that had come through from Mike.

555-330-8004: Think I can see you around 1?

Damn, I had to give him points for being direct. Up until that text he'd been keeping it pretty cordial. He must've sensed that I wasn't with the bullshit when I started dishing out one-word responses.

Me: In the morning?

555-330-8004: Yeah. Unless that's a problem?

Me: It's not.

555-330-8004: Bet. See you then. Frazee Spa & Hotel. Room 1007. I'll leave a key at the desk. What's your real name?

Me: What makes you think Tracey's not my real name?

I looked up from the phone and caught him smiling down at his before he looked up at me too.

555-330-8004: You don't look like a Tracey. And they're gonna ask for your ID. Frazee don't fuck around like that.

I took a deep breath as if telling him my real name would make a difference in what was gonna go down either way.

Me: Melody Bledsoe.

555-330-8004: Got it. Nice to meet you, Melody. (smiley emoji)

He left a smile emoji. And I absolutely hated niggas who sent smile emojis.

Me: I bet it is…

The fake pout that crossed his handsome face as he read that message almost made me feel bad. But then I remembered, this nigga was standing right next to his girlfriend planning a whole smash-session with another woman. He didn't need pity. What he needed was his trifling ass kicked.

Unfortunately, all I could offer him was some good pussy.

II

Mike

I thought I'd never get rid of Kelsey. Didn't give a shit about either of the outfits she'd purchased with my credit card since she'd rather die a virgin than let me pull them off of her.

And I mean that literally.

I was dating the only thirty-year-old virgin in the state of Texas and worked too closely with her father at his car dealership to break things off like I wanted to. She was the kind of boring that made you yawn in the middle of sentences. Lived a superficial life where colors had seasons and being invited to brunch meant you'd survived some kind of unspoken quarterly friendship purge. The only good thing about Kelsey was that she went to bed early every night to avoid sleep deprivation wrinkles, which worked in my favor on this particular night because I was in desperate need of some pussy.

And not just any pussy.

Melody Bledsoe's pussy.

A five foot eight-inch thick stack of sexy that had grabbed ahold of my eyes the moment she walked into Kendra's party wearing a red maxi-dress that silhouetted her curves like a fresh paint job on a brand new Maybach, with no panties underneath from what I could see. I couldn't believe I'd never run into her before, seeing as Kendra and Kelsey had been friends for a minute. Granted, Melody and Kelsey did seem to be from different sides of the track, one being caviar bred while the other was the beautiful product of cornbread and collards. You'd think having a mutual friend in common, they would've at least sat at the same table during one of those meaningless brunches.

Whatever the case, the churning in my groin hadn't been for naught, and Melody dropping her number in my pocket was a welcome surprise. I'd already drummed up five minutes' worth of fantasies before we brushed shoulders in the hallway. And now I was standing in a hotel room, still fully dressed, wondering how hard karma would kick me in the ass for cheating on my uptight girlfriend.

The clicking of the doorknob took my eyes away from the window I was staring out of, night sky providing the perfect backdrop to the hidden escapades that were about to take place. I turned around with my hands shoved in the pockets of my sweats, heart beating like a drum and pulsing in my ears as she stepped in wearing a pair of high-heeled red sandals, low-rise skin-tight jeans pulled into a wedge up the split of her pussy, and a white T-shirt tied in a knot at the small of her back, nipples hard as pebbles beneath the thin fabric.

Melody was fine and she knew it. Walked like it. Talked like it. And from the spread of her hips and the plumpness of her pussy, I was willing to bet my six-figure salary that she fucked like it too. Those juicy ass lips had curled up into a smirk. Apparently, I was taking too long to respond to her presence. But I couldn't help it. My dick had gone from soft to stone in a matter of seconds and I wasn't sure I could step forward without cracking it in half.

"Hi. You look… *comfortable*." Her sexy voice was just above a whisper as she pulled the door closed behind her and stepped in, dropping the keycard and her purse on the side table.

"And you look…" I shook my head because I wasn't sure there was a word in the English language that could accurately describe how good this woman looked. *"Edible."* was what came out. And I knew that it sounded lame the moment it left my lips.

But, "Good." was her response. "That's what I was going for." She smiled—barely. I'd come to notice in the short time that I'd *"known"* her that smiling wasn't a thing Melody did often.

And walking wasn't a thing she did either.

No, she glided. Moved as if there was music playing in her ears and she was staying in rhythm. Perfectly manicured feet led up to thick toned legs, led up to wide enticing hips, led up to a slim waist and a flat belly that I couldn't wait to plant kisses on. Full c-cups laid perky and free from restraint beneath her shirt. My mouth watered at the silhouette of tight nipples that I intended to suck until I was satisfied.

"You thirsty?" I asked, finally willing my feet to move toward her in route to the kitchenette.

"Nope." She replied, looking up into my eyes as I stopped right in front of her, heat circling between our heaving chests. "I didn't come here for refreshments."

"Oh yeah?" I dragged my gaze down her frame, lingering at her ample tits before returning to her eyes. "Then what'd you come here for?" I asked a stupid question, the warm scent of her breath occupying the inch of space between us.

Her big eyes swept to my crotch before slanting back up at me, void of questions or playfulness. The next thing I felt were her soft hands underneath my shirt, traveling the spread of my collar bone, over my chest and down my abs, staying there as she carefully studied the divide of my muscles as if she was committing them to memory.

And then one hand went lower, tracing along the V beneath my waist, still staring into my eyes with heated intensity as she spit into the palm of her hand then slid it down and curled it around my erection.

"*Somebody* knows why I'm here." She licked her lips, hypnotizing me, giving me no choice but to stumble forward as she stroked me long and hard.

"What's wrong, Mike? You feelin' guilty?" She asked.

Still stroking me.

Still staring at me.

Still hypnotizing me with her presence.

"I promise I won't tell." She damn near purred as my eyes fell closed in response to how tight and warm and wet her grip was around me.

"I just wanna fuck you. I wanna fuck you so bad." She confessed. My eyes slowly blinked open just wide enough to see her biting down on her bottom lip, pumping me faster and harder until I almost came.

And then she released me, pulling her hand from my pants, still planted in front of me as she rolled my shirt up my abs then my chest, hard nipples pressing against my stomach as I raised my arms and she reached up to pull the shirt off over my head.

"Sit." She pointed to a chair against the wall behind me, and I backed my way to it with her mimicking my every step.

Long crimson nails shoved into my chest sending me falling back into the oversized suede sitting-chair. I parted my knees and she stepped between them, putting her denim-covered pussy right in front of my face. With no armrests to lay my arms on, I let them hang to the side, awaiting further instruction.

"You like that?" Her juicy lips remained parted as she stared down at me, pulling the seam of her jeans up between her split, forcing a wide wedge between the lips of her pussy.

"You like looking at that fat pussy, don't you, Mike?" She teased, pulling the seam deeper, lips opening as she rolled her hips, visibly aroused as her nipples grew even more pronounced beneath her T-Shirt.

"You wanna taste it?" She slid her hand inside her pants, dipping a finger into her pussy, the scent and sound of her arousal making my fucking mouth water.

"Say it." She urged. "Tell me you wanna taste my pussy."

"I wanna taste it. Please, let me taste it!" I begged. *Begged* this woman whose real name I wouldn't've known if I hadn't tricked her into giving it to me.

She moved forward, digging her knee into my crotch until it almost hurt. Then she pulled a finger out of herself and pressed it against my lips until I hungrily opened my mouth then sucked off every ounce of her nectar, pleased with the sweet taste of nothingness I'd found.

"What does it taste like?" She leaned closer and breathed into my mouth, bathing me with a warmth I didn't even know existed.

"You taste amazing." I panted. I could hardly catch my breath.

"For real?" She grinned and I nodded *yes*.

"Lemme see." She slid her hand back into her pants and started fingering herself.

"Oh..." She moaned, eyes falling closed and shoulders bending forward as her belly caved and she rolled against her palm.

I pulled my dick out over the waistband of my pants and watched, knees falling to the side as she stood between my legs and played with her pussy, titties jumping as tiny convulsions jolted through her body before she finally bent forward and rested a free hand on my shoulder.

"Fuck!" She said more to herself than me, sliding a handful of soaked fingers from between her legs, pulling them to her lips and licking them all clean while I watched with a hard dick in my hand.

"You were right." She trailed off, licking the last of her fingers with a smile on her face, retrieving a condom from the back pocket of her jeans before peeling them off and kicking them to the side.

Standing before me naked from the waist down except for those heels, she ripped the condom open on the first try, bending forward and sheeting me just as quickly and discarding the wrapper on the floor beside the chair. Straddling her legs on either side of my thighs, she sank down over me slowly, soft moans matching mine as her hands found their way to the rise of my shoulders, bracing herself as she slid up and down my length, recreating the same rhythmic speed that she'd walked in on. I gripped her hips, following her lead instead of taking it from her, toes curling in my J's as she gripped my dick, pulling away my desire to do anything but let her. I could feel her thigh muscles tensing, heeled feet planted firmly in the carpet giving her the advantage of full control as she rolled her hips back and forth, sending her breasts bouncing freely beneath her shirt.

"You feel so good in my pussy." She breathed, walls contracting around me, ass sliding up and down my lap, sweats providing a soft barrier between our skin. "I knew you would." She pulled her bottom lip between her teeth, staring at me with those sexy ass eyes, pussy slippery and wet as she lapped it over me again and again.

Having resisted temptation as long as I could, I leaned forward, bending my neck to suck those still covered nipples one by one, leaving two wet circles on the front of her shirt. She arched into me, hips waving back and forth as she took me in deeper, digging her nails into my skin. I pulled her belly flush against my abs, thrusting upward so hard that she screamed out in response to the pressure being applied to the very core of her sex. My head fell back against the chair, teeth digging into the hot skin on my bottom lip as climax threatened to ravish me and render me defenseless to endless sensations. Groin tight, balls heavy, head spinning on an axis of pleasures unknown, I grunted and pumped into her harder and faster, roping my arm around the small of her back to hold her in place. Her breathing on my neck was a small detail but had a huge impact on the force of my stroke.

"Shit!" Shot from my mouth as she wrapped her legs around my waist, tightening around me in more ways than one.

Melody was fucking me. Taking my mind on a trip with her tits smashed against my chest and her wet lips painting the side of my neck, panting her way through this intense exchange of forbidden energies that would no doubt, leave me a changed man.

It felt like I was falling into the floor as the heaviness weighing in my center started to descend to the throbbing muscle between my legs.

Between *her* legs.

Between *our* legs as she squeezed tighter and rolled her hips faster and sucked my neck to pacify the screams that would've likely thrown me over the edge.

Which was where I went anyway.

When my entire body temperature rose to a level that would've been dangerous under other circumstances. I could literally feel the heat from her thighs wrapped around me building a force-field, warding off everything but the need to come undone.

Inside her.

Or on her belly.

Or between those juicy ass lips that would look beautiful beneath a thick load.

But there was no time for that.

Not with her riding me this hard. Not with me sliding in and out of her so fast, feeling so fucking good that I'd forgotten my girlfriend's name and probably my mama's too.

Bliss was the dampness of Melody's ass beneath my palms. I had to slap it to make sure I wasn't dreaming. To remind myself that I was inside a building.

Inside a room.

Inside a woman who had the potential to fuck up my whole world because the pussy was just that good.

"Mike!" She moaned into my ear. And the sound of her voice mixed with the softness of her lips barely grazing my neck was the cue my body needed to spiral. To betray be my losing total control and exploding between her legs.

Melody

I could tell he didn't want me to go. Mostly because he'd said it, but also because he was standing directly in front of me with a hard dick in his hands as I sat on the toilet emptying my bladder.

"Can I help you with somethin'?" I looked up into a set of deep brown eyes that had probably never seen a bad day.

The thick muscle resting against the inside of his thigh was just an added bonus to the privilege he'd been born into. It seemed unfair to be rich, *and* fine *and* blessed with good dick. If the niggas from around my way even heard about a nigga having it this good, they'd kill him out of spite.

Without speaking, he started to stroke himself, smiling down at me, still drunk with lust, grabbing ahold of his dick and pushing the head against my unexpectant lips. I opened my mouth and took his warm flesh in, the medicine taste of the rubber he'd just discarded in the waste-basket still present but not so strong that it would discourage me from sucking him dry.

The first stroke was hard. So hard that my eyes bulged, my gag reflexes were activated, and my stomach caved, threatening to empty its contents all over his golden brown shaft. He slid out to admire the tears welling in my eyes, smiling again as if he'd accomplished something. Then he was in my mouth again, so deep that his pelvis was smashed against my lips.

I gagged as spit curdled in my cheeks, eventually overflowing from my mouth since I was unable to swallow with the head of his penis obstructing my throat. Mike braced a palm at the back of my head, holding me in place as he raised to the tips of his toes and fucked my face with no restraint or consideration for my need to breathe.

"Fuck!" He nearly whimpered, banging against my slippery lips, his length covering the bed of my tongue and filling my mouth to capacity. I strained to keep my eyes open, turned on by the helpless look on his face. My fingers slid down the skin of my caved belly, finding their way to my pussy and entering.

With my legs spread as wide as they'd go, the sides of my thighs touched the chrome toilet paper dispenser on one side and the open space beside the bathtub on the other. I rolled my hips, violently fucking myself as Mike ravished my hot, wet mouth. He braced his palms against the wall behind me, propping a foot up on the side of the bathtub, staring down into my teary eyes and laying into my painfully stretched mouth until it became too much to handle and his eyes shot up to the ceiling.

"Melody!" He screamed my name, shoving into my mouth, sending my head darting backward from the force of his stroke. "Fuckin shit!" His melodic voice shivered, thighs visibly straining to remain standing until the end.

My jaw tightened, strained from being open so long, and my toes curled up onto their tips as an orgasm ripped through my belly trailing a heated inferno. Moaning and stroking and dropping a hand back down to brace against the back of my head, Mike panted his way through a stream of hard strokes before be surrendered to my tight mouth wrapped around him like a suction cup, and exploded between my lips, filling my mouth with his spend.

I opened to let his creamy white load run down my chin, neck, and chest. He backed away, leaning his shoulder against the wall behind him, trying hard to catch his breath as I stood from the toilet, smearing his cum all over my dewy tits.

I smiled on my way to the shower, giving him as little eye contact as possible. I didn't want him to think that this exchange was something that required conversation. He was smitten. Had probably never been with the kind of girl who'd let him do this kind of nasty shit to her body. Little did he know, I'd gone much farther than this. On a scale of one to ten, having my face fucked on the toilet was a weak two and a half.

After a quick shower, I returned to the bedroom to find Mike sitting on the edge of the bed naked with his pretty face lit with questions. Questions I didn't have the time nor the desire to answer. It was already after midnight, and I had an early morning ahead. If Mike was interested in pillow talk, he needed to call up his bougie ass girlfriend.

"Hey, I know you know my situation and everything. But I was wondering if—"

"I already told you your secret's safe with me." I cut him off, collecting my jeans from beside the chair where I'd abandoned them and pulling them on.

"Nah, it's…it's not that." He stood from the bed, dick slapping the inside of his thigh, visibly hardening the closer he got to me.

This nigga must've been on one of those gas station pills. How the hell was he getting hard so fast?

"I was wondering if maybe…I mean whenever you have time if we could do this again?" He stumbled over his words.

Poor light-skinned nigga didn't know the meaning of a one and done.

"Umm, that's gonna be a no." I didn't beat around the bush in these situations. I pulled on my shirt, picked up my sandals, and headed toward the door to collect my purse. "Thanks though. It was fun."

"Fun? Are you kidding me? You're sittin' on a fucking rainbow." His eyes lit up. He was too corny to be walking around with that much dick.

"I'll be sure to add that to my ratings." I nodded, wearing a sarcastic smirk as I bent over to slide into my shoes.

"You're funny." He tipped his chin, having made it from the wide window on the other side of the room to occupy the space in front of me, still wearing the musk of sweaty sex on his muscular chest.

"Funny and sexy as hell." He added, running that long tongue over his pretty pink lips. "You sure I can't get one more round before you head out?"

See now, he was begging. And I loved me a begging nigga. Made my pussy wet all over again and my nipples perked up like soldiers at attention.

"Pick your poison, Mr. Bright." I dropped my purse on the table and kicked off my heels. "How do you want your last meal?"

"Take them pants off." He bit down on his bottom lip. "And head back to the bathroom. I wanna wet that shirt."

I peeled off my jeans and left them pooled on the floor, hurrying to the bathroom as instructed while he followed close behind me, slapping and squeezing the meaty, bottom of my ass cheeks that the shirt didn't cover. We stopped in front of a long mirror mounted over a double sink. He pressed the front of his ripped body against the back of me, planting a soft, lingering kiss down the side of my neck as he leaned forward to turn on the cold water. Cupping his big hands under the faucet, he collected as much water as he could, then palmed it over my chest before repeating the same steps about three times. By the last time, the front of my shirt was completely soaked. Silhouettes of my dark nipples and areola pronounced beneath the wet cotton pulled Mike's eyes to their reflection in the mirror like magnets. His dick pressed against my back, hard and hungry to be inside me as he massaged my breasts in circular motion, squeezing them together and grinding against my ass. I let my head fall back against his chest, squeezing my thighs together as heat traveled down between them. My shirt inched up my thighs as a result of him grinding against me so hard, warmth from his breath bathing the side of my neck as he took my right earlobe into his hungry mouth.

Seamlessly, he released my bosom to retrieve the condom he'd placed on the soap dish before I sucked his dick on the toilet. He pulled his pelvis back away from me to sheet himself, eyes fixed on our reflection in the mirror, taking a deep breath and allowing his emotions to show all over his face as he slid inside of my body, anchoring deeper than the time before.

"Aahh." I didn't even recognize the voice coming out of my own mouth as his thrust nearly lifted my feet off the floor.

Mike was so long, and thick, and heavy inside my pussy. I bent forward to grant more access, resting my palms on the cold countertop. My nipples, rock-solid, freezing and wet, kissed the smooth surface of the marble sink as they swung beneath me. He gripped me at the rise of my hips, slamming into me hard and fast, rolling his hips rhythmically back and forth, edging dangerously close to my spot. He leaned over me, warm dewy skin casting a shadow of flesh on my back, lips forming a tight 'O' as he plunged into me harder. My pussy wept, sore and throbbing from being spread too wide and fucked too hard. He lifted my right leg and rested it on the counter alongside my palm, and went even deeper, pulling a scream from my lips.

"Fuck!" I cried out, consumed by his stroke, feeling a heaviness expanding in the pit of my stomach before it sank down between my legs.

He had become rooted in me, deep and unrelenting, threatening to undo me with each and every pump. I begged for his mercy as he ravished the inside of me, struggling to maintain balance with him rocking me so hard.

And then his frame began to tense, and his arms tightened around my waist, pulling my ass against him, shortening the pullback of his strokes. Mike collapsed on the back of me, the full weight of his thick frame resting on my body, thighs clapping against my skin as he humped me, shoving his dick so far inside me that I could feel the definition of his head applying pressure to my spot. I could barely breathe in this position, skating so close to the edge of climax that breathing didn't matter anyway. Squirming and panting beneath him, throwing it back at him as hard as I could with my pussy spread wide open being fucked down to the bone. I caught a glimpse of his face when I looked up for a second and witnessed him contorting and coming unglued.

"Shit!" Though the warm liquid shooting from his shaft was contained by a rubber, I could feel it firing from his head like a high-powered water gun.

He slapped my ass hard, claps echoing off the walls. And it wasn't long before the building warmth inside me disbursed and had my shoulders hunching, pussy twitching, and toes throwing up gang signs.

"Oh, oooh!" I whimpered as the wave rushed down my spine and momentarily rendered me defenseless. As I crawled out of it, feeling as light as a feather, I looked up into the mirror finding two well-fucked faces who both knew it was time for this night to end.

III

Lovers and Friends

I

Melody

"The fuck you doin' out at two o'clock in the mornin'? That nigga did you somethin'?"

Aside from Kendra, Olli was my closest friend—closer, actually. More like family. And he stayed ready to fight on my behalf. I'd never let him, though. Knowing how quickly he'd dislocate a nigga's neck without batting an eye, I couldn't have anybody's blood on my hands and cared too much about Olli to put him in that position.

Olli didn't do soft talk, but I knew he loved me as much as I loved him. We'd grown up on the same block, raised by young single mothers who had no idea how to take care of us, leaving us no choice but to take care of each other. It was cool having something like a big brother there to have my back. He'd pick me up in cars that he'd rented from crackheads in exchange for drugs, and fed me when I was hungry and my mama'd neglected to buy groceries because she was too busy figuring out what to wear to the club she attended three nights a week. There were ways for me to make my own money, being a young girl who inherited her mother's curves way too soon. But Olli wasn't having that. Told me out of his own mouth that if he ever found out that I was turning tricks, he'd pay a group of nuns to come pick me up so I could pledge my pussy to Jesus.

"Nobody did me nothin', boy. I was just stopping by to see you on my way home." I told a lie, flopping down on his leather sectional, the scent of weed and incents filling up the tiny living room that had been my place of peace on days when I couldn't find it anywhere else.

"Is that a problem?" I asked as he entered the living room from the kitchen where he'd just warmed up a plate of barbecued ribs—one of his many famous dishes.

"You know it ain't. Just ain't seen you at this hour in a minute." He took a seat next to me, long legs sprouting from a pair of basketball shorts that hung low around his waist, ending in a set of big feet that were always tucked in a pair of white socks and Nike sandals.

"You hungry?" He asked from full, dark lips, smoke swimming off his food as he sat the plate on top of a TV tray.

"Nah, I'm good." I nodded, relaxing my back against the sofa. "You heard from Laurie?" I asked, knowing he had because no matter how many times his mama wound up in jail, he was the first one to visit, accept collect calls, and put more money on her books than she needed.

"Damn, niggas really do talk too much around this mother fucker." He smacked on a piece of meat, licking the homemade sauce off his long, chocolate fingers.

"*Niggas* is my mama." I chuckled. "Called me yesterday begging for money, as usual. She dropped that jewel after I sent a hundred to her Cash App."

"That damn Rene." He shook his head.

"A mess, I know." I sighed.

"Well, we got that in common." He picked up a twenty-ounce bottle of root beer sitting on the floor beside his feet, twisted the cap off and poured half of it into a tall glass of ice that was sitting on the TV tray beside his food. Olli was a street nigga down to the bone. But you wouldn't catch him drinking anything close to alcohol. Mostly because he didn't like the way it made him feel, but also because it had been the cause of his father crashing into an oak tree while driving drunk, ending his life before Olli was even born.

"What's she in for this time?" I inquired, knowing that I wouldn't be surprised by the charges because Laurie'd literally been arrested for everything.

"Prostitution." He sucked a glob of sauce off his thumb. "She shoulda known the nigga was five-O. Ain't nobody in they right mind out here payin' for forty six-year-old pussy."

"Olli!" My brows hiked and I busted out laughing.

"What? You know my mama been ran through." He dropped a bone on the plate, pulling a baby wipe from the dispenser he kept on the coffee table because he was a notorious clean freak.

"I'm not about to play with you." I slid out the rest of my chuckle, shaking my head as he cracked a smile, taking a gulp from his drink.

"Olli?"

"Yeah?"

"I need a favor."

"I already knew that." He slanted his eyes at me, gathering his now, empty plate and heading off toward the kitchen.

I hopped up and followed him, leaning against the door frame of his kitchen entry.

"I need to crash here tonight." I twisted my fingers through the string on the sweats I'd thrown on when I stopped by my place to feed Tuna and grab an overnight bag.

"Did that nigga—"

"Maurice hasn't done anything." I had to make that clear because he knew where me and Maurice lived and would drive over there in a heartbeat to kick his ass.

"He's just…gone a lot. And it's too quiet at the apartment, and you know I can't stand too much of that."

"It's quiet here *too*." He looked up from the steaming hot, soapy and bleachy water he'd prepared for a single dish and a baking pan, crisp tapered fade complimenting his long face, a full beard framing his strong jawline.

"I know, but—"

"You can stay." He cut me off. "Scary ass." He shook his head.

"Thanks." I backed out of the kitchen and headed toward the door to grab my bag from the car. "And I'm not scary!" I yelled from the other side of the door. And I knew he was laughing even though I couldn't see him.

"You can have my bed." I reentered the apartment to find Olli dropping a pillow and blanket on the sofa, kicking out of his slides and sitting down on the couch.

"I am *not* sleeping in that spooky ass room."

"My room ain't spooky. Why you always sayin' that shit?"

"Because it's pitch black and I can't see nothin' in there."

"Well turn on the closet light."

"It's too bright."

"What, you want a night light, nigga?" His voice hiked, making me giggle.

"You don't need to see shit in yo sleep, Mel." He rolled out the covers and dropped a fluffy pillow at the head of the couch. "I'mma be here when you wake up. I ain't goin' nowhere."

I'm not sure if it was his intention or not, but hearing Olli say those words sent me straight back to our childhood. To one of the many times that he came through for me when my stupid ass mama couldn't.

She'd left me alone to go party and stayed out longer than usual. Her car wasn't parked outside our complex, and as always, Olli noticed. He came knocking on the door, all of thirteen years old. And when I didn't answer, he climbed through my bedroom window and found me hiding under a fort made of pillows and blankets attached to the footboard of my bed. All of the lights were off because my mama was one of those people who hated seeing light switches in the upward position. It was one of the only things she paid attention to, and I wasn't taking a chance on an ass-whooping. I'd always been terrified of being alone at night, and she knew this but didn't really care. Guess she figured I was self-sufficient and left me to figure shit out for myself. Sadly, that was how I learned most things. Thank God I didn't die in the process.

Paralyzed by the thought of leaving the fort, let alone walking down a long hallway to get to the bathroom, I'd peed on myself and Olli noticed it immediately after popping his head into the tent. Without speaking a word or looking at me with disgust like most boys his age would have, he backed out of the fort, grabbed a set of clean clothes and underwear from my dresser and handed them to me like he was my father, though he was only three years my senior.

He gave me my privacy, leaving the tent to face the wall. And when I was done, he reached in, grabbed my hand and led me out of my fortress. After making us both a spread—Ramen noodles, chopped green onions and a hand full of shredded cheese—he sat there with me on the worn sofa in our living room, eating and watching recorded soap operas, silently healing wounds that he hadn't inflicted until my mama stumbled in just minutes before sunrise.

"But what if I gotta pee?" I adjusted the strap of my bag on my shoulder, quickly climbing out of my thoughts.

"Use the light from your phone."

"I turn my phone off at night."

"Then turn the mother fucker on."

"You know exactly why I turn it off. Now move and give me the couch. I gotta sit up and grade these papers anyway. You wanna help?" I bumped him with my hip and flopped down on the couch, sliding my bag off my shoulder and pulling out the folder that held my completed lesson plans and a few papers I hadn't graded yet.

"Man, you know I don't deal with no school shit." Olli remained standing, tryna figure out how to force me off the couch.

"It's first-grade math tests." I rolled my eyes up at him. "And I know for a *fact* you can handle that, Einstein."

"I'on't know. I got some pretty fucked up memories about math homework." He shook his head.

"You mean when Laurie almost put you out for not knowing how many apples Timmy had left?" I snorted.

"You damn right." He huffed. *"If Timmy had ten motha fuckin' apples!"* He mimicked his mama, and I busted out laughing with him holding up three fingers.

"She had me feeling stupid, for real." He finally took a seat, accepting a stack of papers from my hand after grabbing an extra TV tray to grade them on.

"Yeah. But look at you now, countin' whole bricks and shit."

"Chill." His lips curved at the corner as he dug through my organizer and located a red ink pen.

Olli had been moving dope since he was about thirteen, and made a pretty decent living doing it. He kept a low profile as he matured in the game, cleaning his money through a handful of small businesses, all operated through his daddy's side of the family because his mama's side was nothing but crooks.

But he didn't like talking about it. At least not with me. Aside from the surface-level stuff like the discounts at his establishments that I regularly took advantage of based solely on the fact that we'd been friends since we were little, I was oblivious to the ins and outs. And I didn't mind. I had issues of my own to lose sleepover. It was probably his way of keeping me safe. The less I knew, the lesser the chances of me getting caught up.

We settled into a silence that only the two of us understood, and we were finished grading papers in less than an hour. I was tired as hell, having been up since six the morning before. It was two a.m. on a Sunday, and I didn't wanna sleep my last off day away.

"You ain't sleepin' on this cramped ass couch. It's bad for your back." Olli stood up, folded our TV trays and put them away after we'd cleared the graded papers.

"Bro, you're six-two and I'm five-eight. Whose back is taking the most punishment?" I got up and slid my bag on the floor beside the couch after pulling out my toiletries.

He sighed and looked at me, rolling a set of sleepy brown eyes that held more sincerity than he let on. "You got a point." He tipped his chin up, dark chocolate skin void of blemishes. "But you still ain't sleepin' on this couch."

"Okay. So, if I'm not sleeping on the couch and I'm too scared to sleep in your dark ass room, then why don't you come sleep in there with me?" I propped a hand on my hip, toiletry bag swinging at waist-level in the other, darting my eyes at him and daring him to tell me no.

"Mel,"

"Don't *Mel* me. Just come on." I waved a hand and headed down the hall toward his room.

The sound of his slides flopping against the faux wood floors let me know that he was giving in…*again.*

Olli

"What's that for?"

I'd grabbed my pillow off the couch and dropped it in the middle of the bed to act as a divider. It wasn't the first time Mel had pulled this *spend the night* shit, and I wasn't about to let what almost happened last time happen again.

"You know damn well what it's for." I stood from where I was bent over the bed to find her stepping out of the bathroom with toothpaste foaming in her mouth.

"You scared I'mma bite you or somethin'?" She lisped, rolling those maple brown eyes as she stepped back in the bathroom to rinse and spit.

"The only person scared of anything in here is you." I sat down on my side of the bed and slipped off my slides. "Now shut up and go to sleep so I can sneak out when you start snoring."

It was hard as hell not to stare when Mel walked into a room. Even under those baggy pajama bottoms, her wide hips swayed like waves and shit. I caught a glimpse of her navel when she reached up over her head to secure a silk wrap on her hair. And her nipples looked like Hershey's kisses beneath that thin tank.

Why the fuck wasn't she wearing a bra under there?

Mel was out here trippin' for real.

"I do *not* snore." Her voice was low and tired and unintentionally sexy. "You must be hearing yourself." She hit the light switch, using her lit phone screen to light the way before she climbed into bed, slid her legs under the covers and rolled over on her side to face me, propping her cheek on her fist.

"Nah." I shook my head, bringing my legs up on the bed and laying on my back, tucking a hand under my head. "I ain't never had nobody tell me I snored." I turned my head to look at her, cinnamon skin glowing like it always did, pulling my thoughts to a place that was completely off-limits.

"Is that right?" She hiked a brow, a few strands of her long, thick hair falling out of the wrap down the side of her face.

"You be havin' women in here now?" Her posture tensed. And she didn't think I noticed but I always did.

There weren't too many things Mel could do without me noticing. When she was mad, she chewed the inside of her lip. When she was sad, she wouldn't say shit. When she was happy, she couldn't stop smiling the goofy smile. And when she was scared, she found her way to me.

That is if I didn't find my way to her first.

I didn't mind being her safety net, because, in so many ways, she'd been mine too. I didn't have the world, but I'd grown up with less than most. And she'd been there through it all, consistently showing me love.

Like the first time we met. She couldn't have been more than six years old when me and my mama moved into the apartment next door. We didn't have much furniture, but we were moving everything alone. No pops around to help, and no friends or family that lived close by.

Mel was sitting on the porch having some kind of tea party with this raggedy doll she'd named Rachel. I'd slow down and glance in her direction, then keep it moving when she looked up. Being nine years old myself, I doubted we had anything in common besides living in the hood. But there was something about the way she talked to that doll that made me wonder if she needed a human to keep her company.

"What's your name?" I remember that squeaky voice asking after me and Mama stopped to take a break on the steps.

I didn't say anything because I didn't wanna look lame, entertaining a chatty little girl in a neighborhood I didn't wanna be in in the first place.

"My name is Melody." She yelled from the table, causing my mama to turn around and look at her through the space between the steps.

"My son don't talk much, baby," Mama said. "My name is Laurie and his name is Oliver."

"Olli." I corrected, looking straight forward at a couple of boys about my age playing catch in a small field that separated our apartment building from the one across from us. "My name is Olli."

*"If my name was Oliver, I'd call myself something else too."
Mel giggled. And at that, I turned around and offered up a smile.*

*A few minutes later, Mama tapped my knee and told me it was
time to head inside. As had been the case in our old place, there
was nothing in the frig, so we were basically heading in there to
pull out blankets and sleep on the floor. As little as she was, Mel
was inquisitive as hell. Of all the things we'd carried into our
place, she noticed that we hadn't packed any groceries.*

*A knock sounded at the door about an hour after me and
Mama turned in. I rushed to answer it and saw Mel on the other
side of the screen door. In her little hands was a plate with four
peanut butter and jelly sandwiches stacked on top. It wasn't much,
but it'd make a turd, and it was the thought that counted.*

*"Miss Bobbi told me to give these to you until your mama gets
her foodstamps." She said. "Sometimes we don't have no food
either. But Miss Bobbi always got peanut butter and jelly."*

*"My mama ain't on no foodstamps. And who the hell is Miss
Bobbi?" In hindsight, I could've been nicer. But at the time, I was
always on the defense. People assumed shit about my mama all the
time, and they were usually right. But as the man of the house, I
couldn't just let it slide.*

*"Her." Mel stepped back and pointed to the apartment above
ours. "I told her y'all didn't have no food. I can take those back if
you don't want 'em."*

*"No! I mean yeah...yeah, we want 'em." I stumbled. Mel was
so damn mature for a little girl. "Look, just don't be tellin' people
my mama's on foodstamps, aight?"*

"Ok." She nodded. "You need some milk?" She asked.

*"Nah, we got water." I backed into the door, nodding my head
before pulling the screen closed and watching her walk away.*

"Go to sleep." Snapping out of my thoughts, I disregarded that
line of questioning, because as much as I cut for Mel, who I fucked
was none of her business.

"So *yes*? Cool." She dropped her hand from under her cheek and laid on her back, powering her cell off and dropping it on the nightstand before pulling the covers up to her chest and forcing her eyes closed.

And thank God.

'Cause it would've taken too much willpower to pull my eyes off her nipples lying so close in this cold ass room.

II

Melody

Oatmeal was the easiest thing to cook for breakfast when we were barely old enough to reach the stove. And if we were lucky, Olli could dress it up with some cinnamon, sugar, butter and pet milk that we usually had to borrow from our neighbor, Miss Bobbi. Me and Olli were always up at the butt crack of dawn, hours our mothers couldn't keep up with 'cause they were passed out from the night before. I missed those days; well, at least the oatmeal. Life was so simple then. Nothing like it was now.

"I hope you didn't just ruin a whole pot of oatmeal." That morning grogginess in Olli's voice and the sly grin on his face when he emerged from the hallway made my heart skip a beat.

But I wouldn't tell him that because he wouldn't know how to take it.

I'd stepped over him as he slept like a log on a pallet he'd constructed on his bedroom floor. I beat him to the kitchen to cook our favorite breakfast, and he never thought I did a better job than he did.

"Boy please." I pulled my eyes back to the pot of piping hot oats I'd been stirring, calming the stupid butterflies whirling in my stomach.

"The best oatmeal you'll ever taste is about to come outta this pot." I tapped the metal spoon on the edge of the pot, dropping a lid on top to keep the oats warm while I waited for our wheat toast to pop out of the toaster.

"I'll believe it when I taste it." He stepped into the tiny kitchen. The front of his solid body brushed the back of mine as he made his way to the refrigerator to grab a carton of orange juice.

"And I like extra butter on my toast." He poked my side on the way out after retrieving two glasses from the cabinet.

And there went those butterflies again.

I really needed to get ahold of myself.

"You pushin' it, nigga." I sassed, rolling my eyes as he laughed, taking a seat at the kitchen table.

"I'm surprised you had oatmeal." I grabbed the ready toast and spread butter on all four slices. "All the oatmeal we ate growing up. You oughta hate this shit."

"And so should you." He slid a glass of juice in front of my placemat, moving his hands to the side as I placed his meal in front of him.

"Guess some things never get old." I shrugged, taking a seat beside him at the table for four.

After I settled in, we clasped hands, closed our eyes and prayed over our meal. I couldn't remember the last time we'd sat at an actual table and had breakfast together. Olli was usually up and on his way before most people rolled out of bed. And it felt good sitting there not talking. Just enjoying warm nourishment and listening to the noise of hood traffic outside his door.

Until "When you gon' answer that man's call?" He had to ruin my solitude with that stupid ass question.

"I saw that five O four area code on your phone. That's him, right?" Olli quizzed, looking up at me from his bowl.

"Since when do we spy on each other?" I leaned my head sideways, dropping my spoon in my bowl.

"Ain't nobody spyin'. And you didn't answer my question."

"You ain't my fuckin' daddy!"

"But *he* is. So, what's the deal?"

Now I'd completely lost my appetite and was ready to go home. I didn't need another lecture from another person who thought my biological father deserved a chance to explain his twenty-eight year absence. Kendra'd tried her damndest to push me in that direction. But I couldn't imagine there was anything this man could do or say that would change how I felt about him.

Which was honestly nothing.

I didn't hate or love him. I never fantasized about having a father present because where I'm from, we didn't see daddies around anyway. All I knew was his name and didn't care enough to seek out him or his family. The way I saw it, it was his job to find me.

And then he did.

With the help of some bullshit Louisiana-Texas pipeline, he found me through some folks who knew my mama from back in the day. Turns out, he'd been locked up for statutory rape since I was thirteen. Apparently, prison releases made some niggas all warm and fuzzy.

Whatever.

"*The deal* is I don't wanna talk about this shit just like you don't wanna talk about having women over here." I pushed my bowl to the middle of the table.

"You know what, get out." Olli stood from the table, grabbed his bowl and headed to the kitchen.

"*What?*" I shrieked.

"You heard me. Get the fuck out." He yelled from the kitchen.

"You come over here with this bullshit knowing damn well that ain't us. You gotta go." He rinsed his bowl and placed it in the left sink basin.

"Olli, I was playing." I got up from the table to join him in the kitchen. "You know I'm just fuckin' with you, right?" I stepped in close to him. So close that I could see up his flared nostrils.

"Right?" I roped my arms around his slender waist, pressing my belly against his pelvis, feeling his dick jump against me.

"Back up." He gripped my wrists and pulled my hands from around his waist. "I got shit to do."

"On a Sunday?" I questioned, tugging his chin, trying to force him to look down at me.

"Yeah." He tipped his chin up out of my grasp. "And it's supposed to rain so you should head out soon."

He hurried out of the kitchen after planting a kiss on my forehead, because niggas love sending mixed signals. I stood there for a minute feeling played and ridiculous for trying to open a door he apparently wasn't standing behind.

"Where you at?"

"I'm at Olli's."

"What, you spent the night again? Melody, you and Olli are too big for this slumber party shit."

My mama—respectfully referred to as Rene because she never wanted me to call her Mama out of fear that it might instantly age her twenty years—could never understand how me and Olli maintained a friendship all these years without it graduating to something else.

Now here I was wondering the same thing.

"You've said that before." I sighed into the receiver. The pots and pans clinking in the background let me know she was cooking and had neglected to invite me as usual.

"Whose son are you cookin' for this Sunday?" I asked sarcastically. At forty-four years old, Rene was a certified cougar notorious for fucking young niggas who only entertained her because they heard the pussy was good.

Guess that was one of the few things I'd inherited from her.

"You got a smart ass mouth, lil girl." She huffed. "And for your information, I'm cooking for somebody my age. You'd know that if you stopped by sometimes."

"And I'd stop by if you weren't always fucking begging." I thought to myself.

But "I know." was what I said out loud. "What's his name?" I asked though I didn't give a shit. He wouldn't be around the next time we spoke so really, what was the point?

"Josh." She answered with a smile I could hear through the phone. "Joshua Shaw, actually."

"Wait, you mean the man who owns the *Chop Shop*? Think he had a side-baby from Miss Bobbi's daughter, Keshia?"

"That's the one!" She damn near celebrated. "And he's divorced now, so I'm not worried about no side-babies."

"Wow. Well, good for you." I flicked imaginary crumbs from under my nails, remembering that I'd called my mama for a reason.

"Hey, can I ask you something?" I sat up straight on Olli's couch. He'd told me to leave, but I wasn't through with him. And he'd have to see me whenever he decided to come back home.

"If this is about that twenty dollars, I already told you—"

"It's not about the twenty dollars, Rene." I shook my head.

"Ok." She returned over the sound of running water. "What's up?"

"It's about my…it's about Greg."

"Lord. I thought we dealt with this already." She sighed and turned the water off. "He was trash, okay? Ain't too many ways to explain that."

"Did you know he'd been in prison the last thirteen years?" I looked at my phone in response to a text coming through from Maurice letting me know that he'd fed Tuna and got his ankle scratched in the process.

I thanked him.

"I didn't." She answered. "But I'm not surprised."

"What, why?" My face scrunched.

"Greg liked young girls, Mel. It was only a matter of time before he fucked the wrong one and got his ass sent to jail. Where is all of this coming from anyway? His people contacting you? Y'all pen pals or some shit?"

This was the attitude she'd taken on my whole life. Belittling anything and anybody who tried to get close to me.

"Actually, *he's* the one reaching out to me," I replied. "Has been for the past three months."

"Oh-*oh*…" was her response. "So y'all talked?" All the background noise stopped. She'd even turned the TV volume down from what I could hear.

"Not really." I grabbed a decorative pillow and dropped it in my lap. "He sent a text letting me know who he was after I sent him to voicemail five times."

"Oh."

"Yeah."

"Does he still call?" She seemed strangely curious. She never had anything good to say about the man, if anything at all.

"Every morning at three a.m." My eyes went to the window beside Olli's front door. I thought it was him outside, but it was just someone passing by.

"Wow!" Rene exclaimed.

"Why wow?"

"I don't know. Greg just never struck me as the persistent type."

"That's probably because he met and fucked you within twenty-four hours. Persistence wasn't necessary." I thought to myself.

"Well, he is," I noted. "But I don't plan on talking to him."

"And why not?"

"Wait, what?" Now I was confused. "Of all people I'd expect you to be on my side."

"Why, because I dogged the nigga out your whole life? I've grown, Melody."

"First of all, no you haven't." We both laughed. "And second, he was a twenty-six year old man fucking a sixteen-year-old girl."

"How'd you—"

"Facebook," I answered the question before she could finish asking. "Apparently the first thing niggas do upon release from the pen is open a Facebook account. And just so you know, I'm not judging you." I said and meant that with all sincerity.

"Judging me for what?" She quipped.

"Umm…for not telling me that I was the product of statutory rape?"

"Oh, girl. That was nothing." She laughed. *Laughed* at the fact that at the age of sixteen, she was impregnated by a grown-ass man. And I knew my mama was wild and was raised by a woman who was even more negligent than she. But she had to feel victimized at least a little. This dude left her to raise a kid alone when she hadn't even been raised herself.

"Nothing? You were a child!" I exclaimed.

"Girl, he thought I was eighteen." She fussed. "You and I both know how early those Bledsoe hips spread."

I'm not sure why I was surprised by anything my mama was saying but I was. And it was breaking my heart.

"Well, whatever. I don't wanna meet him."

"Why not?"

"What do you mean why not? He's a damn pedophile!"

"You are always overreacting. I don't know where you get that shit from." She said dismissively.

"Apparently, not you," I whispered.

"Excuse me?"

Okay, I *thought* I whispered.

"Nothin'. It's… nothin'. I'mma hit you up later." I lied.

"No, you ain't." She read me. "But you might have more than one good reason to talk to Greg. They got money, and I heard his mama died. Maybe she put you in the will or somethin'."

And there it went.

Money was always the motive when it came to this woman. She knew without a doubt that if I had a dollar, I'd throw her a dime. And she was probably the one who gave the nigga my number in the first place.

"Alright, Rene. You have a good one." I breathed out a sigh of frustration.

"Mel—"

"Enjoy your dinner with the barbecue nigga." I slid my thumb across the screen and ended the call just in time for Olli to walk through the door.

Olli

"Them white folks gon' lock yo' ass up for not feedin' that cat."

I saw her car in the parking lot when I pulled up. And I wasn't surprised that she hadn't left because Melody was stubborn as fuck.

"Maurice fed her." She stood from the sofa, walking over and grabbing half the groceries from my hands.

"What're we cooking?" She asked. I peeled my eyes off her behind as she headed to the kitchen wearing a pair of purple yoga pants.

"Mel—"

"I know, I know. You told me to leave." She cut me off, turning sideways to face me after we dropped the bags on the kitchen counter.

"I'm sorry, okay?" She looked up into my eyes. And my heart started beating fast as hell.

"I'm just in a crazy place right now. And being around you makes me feel better."

"You got a boyfriend for that. I can't keep bein' no stand-in. Does he even know where you at right now?" I asked.

I always asked.

'Cause if she was mine, ain't no way she'd be spending the night with another nigga. Not even if the nigga was her friend.

"He knows exactly where I'm at. And I know where he is too." She'd turned away and started putting away the groceries. Mel was probably the only person who understood my need to have everything in its designated place. I wouldn't dare allow anybody else this kinda freedom in my kitchen.

"That's hard to believe." I grabbed a bag of sugar, ripped it open and poured it into the half-empty glass canister that came with a set of three that Mel had bought me as a housewarming gift.

"Why?" She snapped.

"Because," I replied.

"Because what?" She closed the refrigerator after placing the tomatoes on the right side of the crisper where I liked them.

And I declined answering that question, deciding instead to stuff the empty plastic grocery bags in a bucket that I kept under the sink. Shit was getting way too awkward between us and if I didn't shut it down, we were bound to make a big mistake.

"You know how I get down, Olli. This thing between me and Maurice is no different than any other nigga I've dealt with."

I hated that she was so casual about this shit. Like she didn't deserve better than being some nigga's jump-off.

"And you're cool with that?" I asked without thinking. "You're cool with niggas just smashin' and goin' on about their business?"

"First of all, it's my preference." She followed me out of the kitchen into the living room. "And second, are you judging me? 'Cause niggas do it all the time. Hell, I'm sure you do it too. In here tryna act all perfect. You probably went to see a bitch while you were out."

"We ain't discussing what I do or who I do it with. I'm concerned with your safety and apparently, you ain't."

"Oh, so it's my *safety* you're worried about, now?" Her voice hiked. She was all up on me while I situated my pillows.

"You sure you ain't concerned about nothin' else?" I turned around and looked down at a stubborn ass, pretty brown-eyed woman who drove me crazy and had me questioning the dynamic of our relationship.

I'd been warding this shit off since she told me about her first kiss. I wanted to kill the nigga who gave it to her. And not because I was scared that he'd break her heart—which he did. But because she hadn't reserved that privilege for me.

"You talk to ya pops yet?" I changed the subject and backed away, staring at her before I turned my back and headed down the hall to the laundry room.

"No. And I'm not going to." She trailed down the hall behind me.

"And why not? You don't wanna hear the dude out?" I turned the washer on hot and lifted the lid.

"I've heard enough." She walked in and hopped up on the dryer, staring a hole through the side of my head.

"Man, *what*?" I threw my hands up. "You starin' at me like you wanna box. What's the problem?"

"The problem is *you*." She answered as I reached up and grabbed the washing detergent off an overhead shelf. "And don't run off, 'cause I really need to say this."

I let out a deep sigh because I hated heavy shit. Especially coming from Mel because her shit was always the heaviest. Dating all the way back to when she had her first period and was ashamed to go in Family Dollar and get her own pads 'cause the only cashier in the store was a dude from the hood that she was crushing on. Girl had me in the damn store looking lost as fuck, tryna purchase an item I didn't know shit about. Long story short, I bought thirty dollars' worth of assorted maxi pads, and I was so traumatized that I can't even pass by a feminine hygiene aisle at any given store without damn near having a nervous breakdown.

"And don't breathe like that." She fussed, leaning back, resting her palms on top of the dryer and crossing her legs at the ankles.

"Damn, I can't breathe?" I chuckled, pouring a cup full of detergent under the running water.

"I'm tryna be serious." Her shoulders slumped, pretty lips pouting like a big ass kid.

"Alright." I grabbed a handful of clothes from the hamper between the washer and dryer. "Proceed."

She swallowed after poking my side for being an ass, and then her eyes went up to the vent mounted in the ceiling, seemingly rooting herself in her thoughts.

"I thought I had daddy issues." Her eyes stayed up as I alternated between glancing at her and loading more clothes in the washer.

"All the shit I've done. The way I am. I figured maybe I was just subconsciously filling a void or something, like a guest on *Iyanla, Fix My Life*, or some shit. You know?" Her eyes fluttered but stayed up. Like she was talking to herself and I just happened to be in the room.

"Man, you crazy." I chimed in.

"*Probably*." She nodded and smiled.

"But that ain't it." She continued, eyes still up, long, sleek ponytail falling down her back.

"Like, I never wanted a daddy and still don't now. So my little theory doesn't make sense."

"Say, you gettin' at somethin'? 'Cause I'm tryna put this chicken in the oven before the game comes on."

"You know what, Olli, that's rude." She brought her eyes down, pulling her fingers together in front of my face like she was grabbing her own words out of the air. "That's real rude, and I would never cut you off for no damn chicken and foot—"

"I'm fuckin with you, man. Just say what you gotta say." I dropped the last of the laundry in and closed the lid on the washer.

Melody rolled her eyes at me and folded her arms across her chest.

"It's you." She said, blinking her eyes back up to the vent then down to me again.

"What?" I had no idea where she was going with this.

"The reason I can't or won't take any man seriously, including my stalking ass cradle robbing ass father, is because of you."

She spilled that out like it made perfect sense. The problem was it didn't. At least not to me.

"Mel, I'on't know what you tryna say but—"

"I'm tryna say I appreciate you." She cut me off, lip trembling like it did the first time she told me that she didn't think her mama loved her.

"And I know this is coming out all scrambled and shit, but nobody knows me like you do. Not even Rene." Her lip trembled harder. And I didn't know what the hell I was supposed to do.

"I'm not tryna scare you." She uncrossed her ankles, thick thighs spreading, straightening her posture as if she'd somehow sensed my nervousness. "But I don't know how else to say this except to just say it. I'm… I think I'm in love with you, Olli. And I understand if you don't feel the same way. Trust me, I get it. I'm no angel and that's probably a turnoff. But I—"

"We can't." I cut her off. "This ain't an option, Mel. I can't do this with you."

"I know." She nodded, a tear dripping down her cheek. "I'm not good enough." She hopped down off the dryer and brushed past me on her way out of the room.

"It ain't that, man. Come on now." I trailed behind her, wishing I could push a button and make this shit stop.

"Would you stop? It ain't like that." I stepped in front of her at the end of the hallway, halting her steps.

"It *is* like that." She glared up into my eyes, making me feel like the weakest nigga in the world for having to tell her no.

"You can't say it 'cause we're friends and you don't wanna hurt my feelings. But I know how niggas think. And right now, you're thinking I got too many miles. Just say it."

I tried looking left and right, but her eyes kept following me. *"Say it."* She gripped my chin between her fingers and pulled down until I was looking into her eyes.

Eyes that had seen me dead broke and hungry.

Eyes that had witnessed me putting my mother in a bathtub and bathing her because she was too drunk to hold a fucking wash rag.

Eyes that had kept me centered when my world was spinning out of control.

Eyes that held the same sorrow as mine and were the only set to know me…. *truly.*

"I'm not saying that shit." I exhaled. Didn't even know I'd stopped breathing until it was time to breathe again.

"'Cause I don't give a fuck who you laid with. Ain't none of them niggas been good enough or you wouldn't be standing here right now."

She didn't move her hands and I couldn't look away. My heart was beating like a racehorse and all I wanted to do was lean in and take her lips into my mouth.

So, I did.

Disregarding common sense, caught between thoughts of grabbing her face and kissing her or walking my ass away, I chose the former. Because tasting Melody's lips had been the only thing I wanted to do since I was old enough to wanna taste anybody.

In my wildest dreams, I couldn't have imagined they'd be so sweet. Releasing her face to rope my hands around her waist, I pulled her tight against me and continued to swallow her up. The faint taste of cinnamon still lingered on her tongue as I sucked it from her mouth, literally taking her breath away. She arched into me and my dick thumped against her belly. I was too worked up to be embarrassed and from the way she stood up on the tips of her toes and roped her arms around my neck, she didn't mind at all that my shit was as hard as J. Cole lyrics.

"Mel," I mumbled into her mouth, head spinning with a thousand thoughts.

This shit felt way too good.

"No. No talking." She pled, darting her tongue back into my mouth, little body squeezed against mine, so perfect and so right. I slid my lips down the length of her tongue, then nibbled her bottom lip. God knows I didn't wanna stop there, but I had to. Fuck, I had to.

"We gotta stop." I pulled my hands up from around her waist and planted them on either side of her face.

"No. Why?" She whined, bright eyes dimming.

"Cause if we go there ain't no turning back." I kissed her forehead.

"Well can we *go there* first? Worry about all the other shit later?" She tried kissing me again, but I backed away.

"This is how I operate." She said. "I'm not afraid of what may or may not happen. I'm gonna love you either way."

"Yeah, well that's not how it works with me." I protested. "You're my closest friend. Closer than family."

"I understand—"

"But you *don't.*" I slid my hands down the sides of her arms, then rubbed my palm down my face.

"I don't have a backup plan, Mel." I stared at her.

I mean right into her eyes and made sure I wasn't seeing anything else.

Not those tight ass yoga pants that had put the print of her pussy lips on display.

Or that thin ass T-shirt that did nothing to mask her nipples.

Or those plump ass lips that would forever change the way I felt about the taste of cinnamon.

I needed to see my friend so that I could say the right thing and make the right decision. A decision that wouldn't leave us both broken apart after this shit she was trying went south and we no longer had what we started with.

"A backup plan for what?" She looked hella confused. She wasn't used to me telling her no, and I sure as hell wasn't used to saying it.

"Our friendship," I replied. Because that meant more to me than anything.

"You've been like a sister to me damn near my whole life, and I don't know how to see you as anything else."

"Olli—"

"I know. We're grown and it shouldn't be that hard." I spoke up, hands shoved in my pockets. "But I can't mess this up. I can't mess *us* up."

"Well, we're probably gonna be messed up either way, then." She looked down at her feet, then back up at me. "'Cause I can't turn this off."

"You need to try." Came out lower than I'd intended. Mostly because I didn't really wanna say it.

"I have." Her eyes swept up the ceiling, visibly trying hard to hold back the tears.

And why?

Why would she put me in this position when she knew like I knew this shit wouldn't work?

What in the hell made her think that she could possibly have a future with a nigga like me?

"I'm sorry," I said. "I really am."

"No, you're not." She slowly lowered her eyes and shot them at me. "You're not sorry, you're scared. And I get that. Believe me, I do. 'Cause I'm scared too. But what choice do we have?" Her hands went out to either side. I swallowed the lump forming in my throat. I'd be damned if she was gonna have me standing there crying.

"Are we supposed to pretend this conversation never took place?" She continued, stepping closer into my space. "Act like we didn't feel nothin' when we just kissed? Is that what you're asking me to do, Olli? To just walk outta here and go back to pretending that you don't want me and I don't want you? 'Cause I can't do that." She was so close that her breath brushed across my nose, warm and demanding like she was melting something away, voice shivering on every syllable, making my chest feel tight.

"I *won't* do that." She protested, nostrils flared, lips trembling as I stared down into her eyes. "I'm a grown-ass woman and you're a grown-ass man, and we can't keep skating around the fact that we fucking belong together."

"Melody—"

"You can *not* tell me no!" She yelled.

"Would you calm down?" I brushed my hands down the sides of her arms, knowing she wouldn't pull away because my touch was what she wanted.

"I hear you, alright? Damn." I breathed out. "You just gotta give me time."

"Time for what?"

"Time to process this shit. I'm not a fuckin robot."

"And I'm not asking you to be." She grabbed my hand and squeezed it tight. "I'm just asking you to try. To give us a shot. That's all."

We went quiet for a minute, and I took that time to gather my thoughts. If we were gonna do this shit, it was gonna be on my terms, 'cause Mel was way too reckless with the way she was getting down. I never judged her for doing her thing, 'cause she was grown and that was her business. But if she wanted something with me, that whole lifestyle had to cease.

"I don't share." I came right out with it. No beating around the bush. "If we're doing this, it's just me and you. Period."

"So, I gotta get rid of all my hoes?" She curled her lips to the side, staring at up at me playfully.

"I'm serious." I didn't crack a smile. We hadn't done more than kiss and I was already pissed at even the thought of somebody else touching her body.

"Fine." Her shoulders slumped. "And just so you know, I'm on a *hoe drought* anyway. Me and Maurice severed ties months ago."

"Good for him." I sighed, relieved to hear that.

"And what's that supposed to mean?' She grinned, confused.

"It means I'm glad we ain't gotta go into this with me getting on a nigga's ass. Now come on, let's go cook."

"Wait, we can't consummate the relationship first?" She tugged at the waistband of my sweats, pulling me flush against her body, tugging her bottom lip between her teeth.

"And that's the other thing." I pulled her hands up to my lips and kissed them one by one. "My preferred speed is slow," I said, staring down into her eyes. "I ain't goin' nowhere. You ain't goin' nowhere. Why rush?"

"Why rush?" She tilted her head to the side.

"Why rush?" She repeated with emphasis.

"Because I'm horny as hell right now, that's why." She whined. And it took everything in me not to lift her off the floor and wrap her legs around my waist.

"You and me both." I leaned in to kiss her forehead. "But if this is gon' be different. If we're really gonna make this work, we need to go into with straight heads. In other words, I don't wanna hypnotize you with this dick." I glanced down at my crotch and Mel couldn't help but smile.

"Fuck you, Olli!" She punched me in the gut, barely leaving an impression before turning around and heading to the kitchen.

"I'm just sayin'." I rushed up behind her, roping my arms around her waist and lifting her off the ground. "You ain't ready." She squirmed and giggled in my arms as I gave in to temptation and planted a kiss on her neck.

"You better get in here and season this chicken before I show you how ready I am." She slipped away from my hold, turning around with a big smile on her face. Then footed her way to the kitchen, ass jiggling just enough to almost make me change my mind.

Three months later...

III

Melody

"Okay, everybody grab your journals from your cubbies and meet me at the circle. Thirty seconds on the clock. And go!"

Being with these twenty-five little people five days a week was easily one of my favorite things. Their little brains hadn't been corrupted by the worries of the world yet. Their expectations were minimal compared to most entitled adults. And unlike my peers who knew better, they thought I was perfect in every way.

Circle time was my favorite. Mostly because they did all the work while I listened and laughed. But also, because it took place on Fridays, just a few hours before I kicked off my weekend.

Throughout the week, I'd have them journal interesting things that took place at or away from school, and by Friday they had complete stories to share. It never ceased to amaze me how funny these kids were. It was exciting and they loved it almost as much as they loved my candy jar.

I took my place in the center of the circle, sitting Indian style on the floor with the kids all around me holding their journals in their hands. All shoes, including mine, had been left at the door to keep the learning space as clean as possible. And as a learned practice, I provided clean, multi-colored one size fits all grip-socks for the kids every single day, since not everyone had a clean pair to wear to school. I, for one, had experienced the embarrassment of wearing dirty socks to recess when Rene couldn't afford to or didn't have time to do laundry. And I wouldn't let that same thing happen to a child under my care. All I asked was that they dropped their grip-socks in the sock basket on their way out so I could wash them and have a fresh pair available for class the next day.

"Who's going first?" I asked, trying to instill in them the practice of deliberation.

"Jessie!" They all yelled as if they'd already convened without me. It made me proud that they were finally getting it. This classroom did not operate under a dictatorship.

Jessie, the shyest of all my students, had blossomed in the last semester. A big smile pushed her blue eyes into a squint as she stood from her seat, twisting the hem of her bright pink t-shirt between her fingers before releasing it to open her journal.

"You ready, Jessie?" I looked up at her and asked, smiling bright to give her that last boost of confidence.

She nodded her head, *yes*, sandy red afro casting a glow around her caramel face. I'd never seen a little girl with more striking features. She was bound to be somebody someday.

"Go ahead." I nodded, and she started to read.

"Monday, me and my mommy and daddy went to the hospital where I was born at. We got to see the room and everything!"

Her stepmother was a nurse, so Jessie was always telling stories about the hospital, including the one about her birth mother passing away during birth, which was shocking but hard to harp on because she didn't seem sad at all when she shared.

"Tuesday, we ate at my Uncle Josh's barbecue restaurant. He makes the best ribs in the world. He even has a Grand Prize Rib trophy that's taller than me!" She waved a hand over her head, and the whole class said *wow*. Meanwhile, all I'd picked up from that tidbit was that Jessie's uncle was the restaurateur who was currently dating my wayward mother.

The rest of Jessie's week was more of the same. She was from a big family and they all had so much going on. Her auntie was J. Shaw, a popular songstress from straight out of H town. Jessie had been lucky enough to go on tour with her for the first time earlier this year and brought back souvenir T-shirts and cups for the entire campus.

Next up was Timothy Reid Jr., respectfully referred to as Teddy, who always had a week's worth of tales about the messes his dog made and how he had to clean them up. Teddy was an only child and had begged for a Labrador retriever when he realized his parents weren't going to give him a baby brother. And now that he'd gotten the dog, Max, all he wanted was for the pup to come up missing.

I'd learned the hard way to read Teddy's journal twice before putting it back in his cubby. The second week of this exercise he called Max a "shitty son of a bitch". And though I was impressed by the fact that he'd spelled every curse word correctly, I had to sensor him and sit down to have a talk about classroom language etiquette.

After Teddy wrapped up his edited journal entries, a knock sounded at the door and my aide went over to see who it was. Imagine my surprise when a huge bouquet of roses floated in, cradled in the long arms of the most handsome chocolate man General George Elementary had ever seen.

"*Olli?!*" I couldn't help but smile as he stepped into the room with one hand tucked in the pocket of his slightly baggy jeans.

He'd been sending flowers every Monday for the last three months for no reason other than to brighten my day, and it was pleasant to see him show up *with* them this time, and a surprise since it was Friday.

"*Ooooh*, Miss Bledsoe got a boyfriend!" My wild child, Kimberly, was the first to speak. And the rest of the class fell right in line, oohing and giggling as all their little eyes turned to the tall man who'd helped me put together their *First Day of School* goodie bags.

"Simmer down, everybody." I stood up in the middle of the circle, making my way towards Olli for an introduction since they'd never seen him in person.

"Class, this is Olli, my best friend in the whole world. Say hi." I pulled Olli's hand from his pocket and gripped it, fighting the urge to raise up on the tips of my toes and take his lips into my mouth.

"Hi, Olli!" They all sang, and Olli almost blushed.

"Wassup?" He tipped his chin, trying his best to look hard in front of a classroom full of kids who didn't give a damn about his street cred.

"Is Olli your real name?" Teddy asked, and no one was surprised.

"Nah, it's my nickname," Olli replied as I released his hand and rubbed down the center of his back.

"Then what's your real name?" Kimberly stood up and tilted her little head to the side, sending a long black ponytail swinging over her shoulder. "You can't sign in at the front desk without a real name or Officer Saldano will come and drag you outta here kicking and screaming."

"Sure will." Teddy nodded.

"Uh hun." Jessie agreed.

"My real name's Oliver," Olli answered with a smile. "Y'all make sure to tell Officer Saldano I followed the rules, aight?" He hiked a messy brow and made my belly churn.

"Yes, sir!" They all sang again. These kids were something else.

"Can Mr. Olli tell us what he did this week, Miss Bledsoe?" My booger eater, Larry, pulled his finger out of his nose long enough to raise his hand.

And the look on Olli's face was priceless. There was no way he was about to tell these kids that he'd been responsible for astronomical-sized drug deals for a good part of the week. Hell, he wouldn't even share that with me.

"Larry, I'm sure Mr. Olli has to get back to work. Maybe next time." I said.

"Nah, I'm good." Olli looked down the side of his arm into my eyes, handing me the roses and grabbing a tiny chair to take a seat in the center of the circle.

"Lord, I'm 'bout to lose my damn job..." I thought.

Olli

Mel was used to me hustling. I'd been doing it so long, she didn't even ask about it no more. But what she didn't know was that I'd been slowly stepping away from it. I'd recently completed all required courses to receive my associates in Business Management at the local community college and planned to enroll at Phoebe Lee University next semester.

I'd be lying if I said it was gonna be easy stepping out of the game. Though I lived a simple life—too simple by most standards—it was nice having that cash cushion, especially coming from where I came from when most days, we didn't have shit. But it'd be worth it for the trade-off. A life where I didn't have to keep looking over me and Mel's shoulders all the time. Waking up in cold sweats after dreaming about one of my spots getting raided, and worst of all, having my freedom taken away.

I'd rather die than be behind bars.

One of my cousins that had been at it with me since the beginning agreed to take over for me and I trusted him to do well. He was more like me than the rest of the niggas we dealt with. A man of few words who knew how to check a situation without losing his cool. Most cats didn't know, but that was the secret ingredient. Shut the fuck up and let 'em see what you sayin'.

I took a seat in a chair that was ten times too small, knees bent up like I was inside a Cracker Jack box. The kids thought it was funny, so I just went with the flow. It was the least I could do for showing up unannounced.

"Alright, so, check it." I started, and I know Mel cringed. Got my ghetto ass in here talking to these kids like I was about to sell 'em some dro.

"My week went fast. So, you gotta pay attention." I continued, clasping my hands together with my elbows resting on my knees.

"The first thing I do every single morning as soon as I wake up is kiss Miss Bledsoe on the cheek."

"You mean before you brush your teeth? *Ewwww!*" A little girl about Mel's color yelled. Kimberly, I think.

"Yeah!" I smiled, scrunching my brows at the little woman. "So, if Miss Bledsoe ever comes to class with a stinky cheek, you can blame it on me. Aight?" I nodded, giving a thumbs up and they all said *aight* in return.

The rest of my spill was basically about how I had different businesses to check on about three days a week. The laundromat my pops' sister ran, the carwashes my cousins held down and the burger joint I'd opened up with my homeboy, Terry. They were all being used to clean dirty money, but the kids didn't need to know that part. And I couldn't leave out how I talked with Tuna every morning because she was cool for a cat and I kinda liked her company.

"Are you rich, Mr. Olli?" A little caramel cutie with eyes the color of the ocean raised her hand and asked before she was called upon. I knew based on descriptions that Mel had given at home that this one was Jessie Shaw Jr. A little girl named after her pops. That was some cool ass shit.

"He can't be rich, or Miss Bledsoe wouldn't have to work." Kimberly chimed in. This one was gonna be hell when she grew up.

"My mommy said if my daddy wouldna torn his ATL in college, she wouldn't have to work 'cause he'd be in the NFL right now." Kimberly continued, hand propped on her hip, lips pursed like somebody three times her age.

"It's *ACL*, Kimberly. And I think it's time to wrap up." Mel came into the circle and stood next to me, face scrunched and eyes hiked while her aide's face was red from trying not to laugh.

"We're gonna step outside for a minute, Dalia," Mel said to her aide, reaching out a hand to help me up.

"Ok." Dalia mouthed. "Nice meeting you, Olli." She offered a smile before instructing the class to put up their journals after they'd all told me goodbye as I waved on the way to the door.

Melody

"Wait, you're what?"

I knew I was notorious for getting so wrapped up in my own shit that I missed a lot of stuff going on around me. But there was no way in hell this man had completed two years of college without me having a clue.

"Graduating." He repeated. "Tonight. I wanted to surprise you."

"Well color me surprised. How? When? *Where*?" I didn't think my eyes could get any bigger.

School had let out and all the kids filtered out to their bus lines and car-rider lanes, giving Olli high fives on their way out the door. We were heading out of the school after I'd locked up my room and this info had me floored, emotions teetering between overwhelmingly proud and completely surprised. I think I almost fainted.

"Man, I already answered all that." He chuckled, straight white teeth peeping from under those full lips. I wanted to kiss him so bad it made my knees weak. "And you need a new dress."

"*And* shoes!" I added. Because, *shoes*, duh.

"And *shoes*." He shook his head, opening the door on the passenger side of my car to let me in. His cousin had dropped him off so we could ride wherever together.

Olli always spoiled me rotten; more so now that I was lying next to him every night. And speaking of which, I'd never felt so tortured in my life. Being wrapped up in his arms, pressing my behind against his middle. I hadn't dry-humped so much since I first discovered masturbation. I was starting to get migraines and had a sex-deprivation pimple on the rise of my right cheek.

This was all new to me, having a man that saw sex as something worth waiting for. Worth celebrating. Like it was a prize and I was a cereal box. Problem was, Olli's ass wasn't even eating the *cereal*. I knew he loved me. Never doubted for a second that he was as attracted to me as I was to him. But it had been three long months since we started out on this journey and I was starting to wonder if he was having second thoughts.

"Oh yeah, we gotta swing by county and pick up Mama." He added, climbing into the driver's seat as I fastened my seatbelt.

"She didn't get to see me graduate high school. Figured she could make up for it." I slid my eyes back over to Olli who was wearing a prideful grin.

"I am so proud of you." I reached up and stroked his chin. "I don't know how you pulled it off right under my nose, but I'm proud."

"Oh yeah? How proud?" His face took on a sinister stare that made my insides wake up and my nipples solidify.

"Alright now. Don't be asking me that question if you ain't ready for the answer." I rolled my eyes down to my phone, opening a text from Kendra asking if I'd be free for the night.

"Who's that?" Olli asked, eyes on the road as we exited the school's parking lot.

"Kendra," I smirked. "Tryna see if I wanna go to Bottoms tonight."

"Oh yeah?" He signaled right, looking both ways before hopping on the feeder.

"Yeah," I said, scrolling FaceBook before I replied to her text.

"Well, you can go 'head and turn that down." He said, merging onto I-45.

"Oh really?" I chuckled. Olli had never been possessive, and sure as hell didn't give me a hard time about chilling with my girl.

He relaxed against the seat after sliding into the far-left lane, long fingers gripping the steering wheel. It was a damn shame how such a subtle action turned me on so much.

"Yeah. You gon' be busy." He glanced over at me, dropping his free hand on my thigh and pulling it open toward him. I chewed at my lip, staring over into a set of eyes that looked exactly like a cup of steaming black coffee.

"Lemme get a sample." He said, tugging at the zipper of my jeans.

"Right now?" I squeaked. I was beyond fucking shocked.

"What, you scared?" Olli smirked. "I know you ain't scared." He cracked a smile, deep ass voice had my pussy purring in my panties.

"I ain't never scared." I unbuttoned my pants while his eyes went back to the road. "You better not wreck my fuckin' car, Olli." I quickly unzipped and waited for his hand to fall in place.

And it did.

Swiftly and without him even looking, he slid his hand under the waistband of my peach, bikini cut panties. Navigating his way to my pussy without the need for GPS, he rolled the pad of his thumb over my throbbing clit, pulling a moan from my hungry lips.

"You wet as fuck." He glanced at me, long digits sliding inside, making for the perfect fit.

The sound of Meek Mill's "Dangerous" playing on the radio would forever be the soundtrack to Olli finger fucking me on the freeway. My eyes fell closed as I rolled against his palm, bracing my hands on the window seal and center console. Breathing hard, my lips parted, and I squirmed in my seat. A feathering energy circled in my belly, threatening to throw me over the edge in the middle of traffic. Olli's dark eyes slanted between me and the road. He knew exactly where to touch me and for exactly how long. His thrusts were heavy and intentional like he was unearthing something that he'd planted in me. His fingers strummed my sex so rhythmically that it almost felt like a song.

"You like that shit?" He asked, eyes straight ahead, voice low and flowing under the music. "All these people driving past us, and they don't know I'm fingering yo' pussy. That turn you on?"

"Ye…yes!" I whimpered, closing my thighs around his hand. "Fuck, Olli!" I screamed out his name.

"Open 'em up." He commanded, forcing my legs apart. "Let that pussy cum. Don't be scared."

He stroked my pussy faster and his lips tensed up. And I could see an erection growing under his jeans.

"Shit!" I reached across and gripped his dick through his pants.

"I want you so bad right now." I stroked him while he stroked me.

"Can we pull over?" I begged, climax snaking between my legs.

"Olli, *please*!" I slid my ass back and forth against the seat, quickly realizing that even if he did pull over, I'd be cumming before he could.

My shoulders bent forward and my belly caved. Pelvis whirled with electricity that was beyond my control. Gripping his flesh in my hands, I bent forward and closed my thighs. With the power of his upward thrust, tapping at my spot with perfect precision, my body fired off on all ends and I came completely unglued.

Shivering aftershocks were the only indication that I hadn't died on gone to Heaven. I opened my eyes in the wake of my orgasm to find Olli licking his fingers then turning up the music, winking at me because the slick mother fucker knew exactly what he'd done.

IV

Olli

It was disappointing but no surprise that my mama was already gone when I made it to the jailhouse. She'd pulled the shit before; hopping in the first thing smoking and turning her first trick in the backseat of some nigga's car before the gates of the prison closed behind her. Most would be pissed, and Mel definitely was. But I'd grown immune to it. This woman had been letting me down my whole life. It was fucked up, though. A new low, even for her. She missed my high school graduation because she was behind bars. And now she'd missed my college graduation because somebody beat me to the gate on her release date.

"You sure you're okay?" Mel asked on our way to a secret location. "We can go home. We don't have to do all this."

"I'm good. For real." I pulled her hand up to my lips and kissed it. Nobody looked better riding shotgun in my ride. We were gonna spend the rest of the night forgetting about all the bullshit.

"Besides, we need to finish something," I said.

"Oh yeah?" Her brows hiked.

"Hell yeah." I signaled right, heading into the boat docking area at Kemah Boardwalk.

"Where you goin'?" Mel sat up straight in her seat. "Olli, these people are gonna have us arrested. You can't just be parking out here. Did you read that sign?"

"I just graduated college. I think I can read a sign. Come on." I hopped out of the car and went around to her side. I pulled the door open and this crazy-ass woman refused to get out.

"What are you doing?" She looked up to the side at me, face tense with concern.

"Man, just get out the car." I extended my hand. "It's a surprise, and you ruinin' it right now."

She rolled her eyes, grabbed her purse, and allowed me to take her hand. "Alright." She smacked her lips. "But if this is some drug shit—"

"Mel, seriously?" I whispered, though nobody was in the parking lot but us and a small party of drunk white folks.

"Just bring yo' crazy ass on here. Shit." I helped her out of the car, quickly remembering why I'd gone through all the trouble of putting this night together the minute I saw how that dress was hugging her ass.

"I'm just sayin'." She fussed, walking alongside me, heels clacking against the pavement. "I watch a lotta dope dealer shows. And they always wind up getting into shit around water. It's typically not a happy ending, is all I'm saying." Her eyes were darting all around. Up to the lights that illuminated the lot, and around at all the boats and yachts docked in the waterway ahead of us.

When we made it to the entry of the docks, an older man about a shade darker than me—which technically made him blue— approached us holding a tray with two glasses of champagne on top and a set of small cards with our names on them. His name was Bertrand Senegal, and I'd been talking to him for the past month about putting this whole thing together. He was solid from what I'd gathered. I was rarely wrong about shit like this.

"Mr. Black, it's a pleasure to see you again." He greeted with a thick Caribbean accent, offering a firm handshake and a smile.

"And this beauty must be Miss. Bledsoe." He gestured for her hand. When she extended it, he planted a kiss on top and I had to remember where I was.

Mel's face was stuck between excited and confused as Mr. Bertrand released her hand and offered a flute of champagne. She accepted it, widening her eyes at me to see if I'd do the same since I didn't drink. Little did she know, both glasses were filled with Sparkling Rosé Grape Juice. We'd both be in our right minds tonight.

"Excuse my manners, Miss. Bledsoe. My name is Bertrand. *Captain* Bertrand if you're into formalities." He offered after we'd taken our drinks from the tray. "My family and I will be at your service this weekend. Let's head on over to *Lou Anne*."

"Nice to meet you! Mel is fine. And who is Lou Anne?" Mel asked, falling in step as I took her by the hand and followed Bertrand.

"Our yacht." Bertrand laughed. "Looks like Mr. Black kept good on his promise to keep all of this a secret!" He looked back over his shoulder and winked, salt and pepper locs braided and hanging down the middle of his back.

"Yes, he did." Mel looked up at me as I pulled her hand to my lips.

"You mad?" I leaned to the side and whispered in her ear, taking a second to nibble it 'cause I knew she liked that shit.

"No." She flicked her tongue out, shoulders hunched as she shuttered against the side of me. "Just surprised...*again*." We halted our steps as we made it to the middle of the dock and Bertrand opened the entrance to the yacht.

Melody

Beautiful was an understatement. This yacht was exquisite. We hadn't even made it past the entry yet, and my mouth and eyes were wide open. Caribbean music played from a sound system overhead, and soft lighting surrounded the deck and upper level. I didn't see any food yet but the smell of *jerk something* was floating through the air on top of the breeze.

I didn't realize how tight I was holding onto Olli's hand until he leaned in and asked if I was ok. I nodded *yes*, planting a kiss on his cheek as we followed Bertrand around to the other side of the yacht, and I prayed that wherever he was leading us, there was a plate of food nearby.

Out on a deck facing the water stood two beautiful brown women dressed in black pants and white, long sleeve collared dress shirts. One looked to be in her late forties, though she could've been eighty 'cause black don't crack. And the other was much younger but had the same round face. Both of them wore long black locs pulled into neat buns at the back of their heads. They were absolutely gorgeous and smiling from ear to ear, apparently glad to be of service to me and my handsome beau.

"Hello, Mr. Black and Miss. Bledsoe." They greeted us with the same kind smile as Bertrand.

They introduced themselves as Trini, the younger woman, and Eralia, the older lady, before showing us to our seats at a table for two. A vanilla-scented candle flickered from inside a colorful bouquet of assorted flowers at the center of the table. They'd paid attention to every detail with the décor, right down to the crimson ribbons wrapped around the back of our seats. In front of us lay beautifully engraved menus with mouthwatering descriptions of the three-course meal we'd be dining on. Olli had taken it upon himself to pick out everything, right down to the dessert. And I trusted his taste without wavering because a man who could cook was obviously a man who knew what to feed me.

Our appetizers were Callalo patties with a flaky dough that made it hard to stop at one. But Olli warned me that if I went too far, I might not have room for the entre. And I'm glad I listened because when Trini and Eralia pulled the lids off the dishes they placed in front of us in synchronization, my mouth started watering and I might've even drooled. Steam swam from a plate of braised oxtails, a meal I hadn't had since our neighbor, Miss Bobbi cooked it, and she'd never prepared them with these spices. Marrying sweet and spicy with such perfection that I had to close my eyes to chew, the meat was so tender it melted in my mouth. I was sitting there having a foodgasm.

By the time we reached the bottom of our plates, there was definitely no room for dessert. So, Olli asked that it be brought down to our rooms after we'd freshened up and settled in. Bertrand gave us a grand tour of the spacious yacht, including the pool on the backside that I didn't see when we came on, and a dance floor behind it that could've easily provided enough space for a small party. I'd never seen Olli do more than an almost undetectable two-step at local house parties. But apparently, he was feeling himself that night and wanted to dance before we headed to our room.

"I'm glad you wanna do this before we head out into the water." I reached up and roped my arms around his neck as he pulled me in against him and wrapped his arms around my waist.

"Why you say that?" He leaned back and squinted, knowing I was about to say something smart.

"'Cause you can't dance, that's why!" I giggled.

"What makes you think I can't dance?" He squeezed me tighter against him, applying pressure to the small of my back with those big ole hands.

"I've never seen it." I returned, lashes fluttering, breeze blowing through the flowy fabric of my long, yellow dress.

"Well, I guess you gotta trust me." He slipped an arm from around my waist, taking one of my hands and angling it to the side.

"Do you trust me?" He leaned into my face, the scent of dro and Caribbean spices lingering on his warm breath and dancing across my lips, sending tingles down my spine.

I nodded *yes*, unable to speak as Olli leaned in and planted a lingering kiss on the bend of my neck. He led our bodies from side to side, swaying with our centers pressed dangerously close together. I could feel his heart beating in synchrony with mine. I had never felt more in love with him than I did in that moment.

The song playing, "Ways" by David Meli, was mellow but definitely offered space for some dirty whining. Olli had turned into a man I hardly recognized, rubbing against me and slowly moving his hips, maintaining his gangster while giving hints of what he was capable of putting down in the bedroom. I mirrored his movements, arms quickly finding their way back up and around his neck. He secured his long arms around my waist, fire shooting from his eyes straight into mine as he pushed his knee in between my legs. I ground against him, pussy throbbing as he controlled the whirling of my hips by sweeping his knee from side to side. He awoke the dormant depths of my sex and pulled them to the surface like no one ever had before.

Just as I started to feel him coming alive in his pants, he spun me around until I was facing the water and pulled me back against his chest. The frame of his solid body felt so safe and warm. Hands squeezing and caressing my ass, setting my skin on fire. I melted to pieces right where I stood, falling deeper in lust with his lips planted on my neck again.

"You feel that?" He whispered in my ear, grinding his erection into my ass.

"Yeah." I almost purred, so hot, I could've burned a hole through the floor.

"You wanna take care of it?" He whispered, grinding into me harder, in keeping with the rhythm of the music.

I peeped over my shoulder, looked straight into his eyes and nodded *yes* as he kissed me long and deep, only pulling away to nod at Bertrand and let him know that we were done dancing for the evening.

Olli

Bertrand had hooked it up. I mean really hooked it up. And I know I'd paid a grip for all this, but he'd exceeded my expectations from the welcome to the dinner and the all-around service. We didn't have to lift a finger, and more importantly, that smile hadn't left Mel's face.

Originally, I'd planned on having both of our mamas on board since they'd never experienced anything like this. But when my mama pulled that shit, it didn't feel right inviting Rene since she'd likely be entertaining herself once me and Mel went down to our room. It worked out for the better, though. We had more time to focus on us. Besides, I hated sharing her anyway. We'd have a lifetime to focus on that.

"Can we live here?" Mel walked out of the bathroom with her hair free from the band that had been holding it in a ponytail all day, wearing a peach-colored nightgown that fell just below her behind.

I grinned from my spot at the foot of the bed, resting my elbows on my knees having changed into a pair of pajama bottoms. I couldn't believe I had her all to myself. My mouth watered at the thought of all the shit I was about to do to her.

"Why you grinnin' so hard? Silly ass!" She giggled, hips swaying, nipples tight as she sashayed in my direction.

"Do you know how fine you are?" I replied, having no issues being completely honest with Mel. This couple shit had finally grown on me.

"I do. But why don't you tell me." She pulled her bottom lip between her teeth, stepping between my open legs, putting her barely-covered pussy right in front of my face.

"Good enough to touch." I gripped her ass and she planted her palms on my shoulders.

"Good enough to squeeze." I massaged her cheeks, loving the way her soft flesh felt beneath my fingers.

"Good enough to eat." I pulled her in closer, rolling her gown up to expose her un-pantied sex, breathing in the sweetness of her musk, dying to have her inside my mouth.

I looked up into her eyes, catching a hungry stare that let me know she wanted to be tasted. My mouth watered, dick painfully tightened between my legs. I had to reach down and grip it, using my free hand to spread her folds, glistening wet pinkness all mine for the taking. I circled my thumb over her clit, pulling a moan from her cords as she arched into my palm, thighs spreading to grant full access.

"Ooohhh!" She moaned, contracting around my finger as I slid it inside her, stroking myself while watching her come undone, the tortured expressions on her face forcing me to go harder.

Feeling her knees tremble as her legs spread open against the inside of my thighs, I planted my face between her legs and swiped my tongue up her split, bathing the contours of her pleasure. It was too much yet not enough. And I had a feeling it would always be this way. She rested her hands on my shoulders to brace herself as I went down on my knees and pulled her over my mouth. She spread her legs wider as I darted my tongue in her pussy, following the wave of her hips rocking back and forth over my face. She tasted like heaven, clean, and wet, and perfect, moaning inaudible words of satisfaction as I tried my best to eat her alive. A sweet smell that was all her own seduced me into sucking her nub into my mouth until it was swollen, red and warm to the touch. She slipped and slid over my face, sliding her pussy up and down my lips, using me and bathing me with her sweet juices, leaving me no choice but to drink them up. I came to a swell inside my own hand, dick threatening to explode at the sound of her voice crying out. I reached up and gripped her hips, making her grind against me harder until climax ripped through her body and I had to hold her there in place.

Melody

Head down, ass up, and completely out of breath, I watched from the corner of my eye as Olli retrieved a condom from the dresser behind us. I'd been imagining his dick for a long time. What it would look like. What it would feel like. Even how smooth it would taste laying hard and warm against my tongue. But nothing had prepared me for the dark chocolate, pink-tipped, long and thick muscle hanging down the inside of his thigh as he approached me from the back, setting my whole body on fire.

Outside the bedroom, Olli wasn't much of a talker, and I didn't mind because his vibe made up for it. But in the bedroom, he was extremely vocal. He liked it loud, and descriptive, and nasty as fuck. And I could dig that. That was right up my alley.

"Spread ya legs." He tapped me on the ass, holding his dick in his hand like the deadly weapon it was.

And I did as I was told, deepening the arch in my back until my belly kissed the mattress. I wanted to feel him inside me so bad I could hardly regulate my breathing.

"You always this wet, Melody?" He said my whole name, deep voice stimulating parts of me that had never been awakened, dipping a finger inside my pussy and whirling it around.

"No," I told the truth, though it was hella embarrassing. I had to concentrate on other things around Olli or my pussy would *stay* wet.

"So that's for me?" He asked, still teasing me with that finger.

"Yes." A whimper of desperation left my lips.

"Say that shit." He commanded. "Say *'my pussy is wet for you, Daddy'*."

The authority in his tone sent chills up my spine. My nipples pebbled, heart skipped a beat, and my pussy contracted around his finger. I ached for his entry. Didn't have room in my mind for anything else. And as he stood behind me, finger deep in my pussy with his big hand palming my ass, I followed his command without hesitation because I needed him so bad.

"My pussy is wet for you, Daddy." I purred, praying that would be enough to pull him inside me.

"Louder!" He yelled, smacking my ass so hard it stung.

"My pussy is wet for you, Daddy!" I shouted louder. But not as loud as I could because something deep down inside of me wanted him to smack my ass again.

On the overhead speaker, Capt. Bertrand announced that we'd be setting sail in the next few minutes. I didn't give a damn if the world was about to end, I wanted Olli in my pussy, safety precautions be damned. And he must've felt the same, disregarding the announcement, smacking my ass cheek so hard that I swear I saw stars. On his command, I screamed again, having taken all I could. And before I could finish screaming, Olli was pushing inside of me.

"Shit, Melody!" His pelvis clapped my ass. So thick and wide, he was massaging my walls, buried deep, deep inside, damn near touching the bottom.

Body caught between the agony of intensity and pleasure, I scrunched my fingers into the soft, white comforter, and rode the wave of Olli's thrust. He felt good, and hard, and all-consuming inside my pussy. Like everyone who'd ever been inside me before was simply trying to take his place.

But they couldn't.

Not with the way he was swelling against my walls, holding my ass cheeks open, surging in and out of me, applying pressure that graduated to pain before he pulled out and soothed it.

My titties smashed into the bed as he forced me to arch deeper, rendering me defenseless to his stroke. My head lay sideways in a pillow that he'd pulled from the head of the bed, laying his long body on top of mine and warming me as he did so.

"Tell me how it feels, baby." He stroked me slowly, craning his neck to stare down into my eyes.

I mouthed *good*, too consumed and filled up with him to be vocal.

"I need to hear you, Mel. Please, baby. Say it." He begged.

"*Good.*" I tried. I really tried. But my pussy was so wide open that I was in a state of disbelief.

Without pulling out, Olli went down onto his back, spinning me around to face him with my pussy still gripping his dick. I assumed that he was as far inside of me as he could go, but quickly realized that wasn't the case when I sat up on top of him and almost cried when he threatened to enter my belly.

"You okay?" He sat up and asked, planting his hands around my waist and lifting me in response to the petrified look on my face.

"I can't ride you, Olli. It's too much." I felt like a big ass punk.

I had never in my life encountered too much dick. But *this*, this shit was long.

"Hold on." He said. "Put your arms around my neck." He directed, and I did what he said, trusting that he had a resolution for this literally *big* problem.

I tensed up a little, balancing the weight of my body on my knees so I wouldn't sink down on him and potentially fucking die.

And then he whispered, *"I'm not gonna hurt you."* looking straight into my eyes. And despite the fact that my pussy was telling me to jump out of the bed and save both of us from being ruined, my heart was telling me that Olli had never done anything but protect me all my life.

So, I relaxed…*kind of.* As much as one could under these circumstances.

"You wanna drive or you want me to?" He asked. And I was all about dominating shit. But not with Olli. With him, all I wanted to do was let him lead the way.

"You drive." I kept my hands roped around his neck, observing him intently as he hooked his forearms under the bend of my knees.

Making me feel as light as a feather, he hoisted my body up, then slowly slid me up and down his length, careful not to go too far, giving just enough to make me moan.

"You okay?" He asked, staring at me as my mouth fell open and my nipples tightened before his eyes. I bit down on my lip, nodding *yes* as he maintained control of the speed and depth of his stroke, supporting the weight of my body on his arms like I didn't weigh anything at all.

"You feel so good, baby." He damn near sang to me, leaning forward and sweeping my lips apart with his tongue, tasting me and sucking me, sending blood rushing to my head.

Try as I might, I couldn't help the urge to reciprocate his strokes, finding just enough give in his hold to rock my hips back and forth. Luckily, he read my body, sucking down the length of my tongue before taking his lips to my nipples and giving each of them the same treatment as he prepared to lay on his back. In this position, it was up to me to control how deep he traveled. I leaned forward and braced my palms on his pecs and slid my pussy back and forth over him.

"Fuck." I moaned, staring down into his eyes, agonizing over the peak that was taking too long to reach. I wanted to cum so bad it hurt. Wanted to feel his warmth popping off inside me. The tension in his handsome face matched the tension in his thighs squeezing together beneath my ass.

Harder and faster I lapped over his girth, wishing I could take it all, but more than pleased with what I could take. Olli gripped my ass and pushed into me, hitting my spot with a sideways stroke that had me convulsing on top of him, and spiraling out of control. I cried out his name, thighs slick with sweat rubbing against his skin. He crashed into me so hard and so fast. And before either of us knew it, we'd surrendered our bodies and fell completely over the edge.

V

Olli

"Get up, *Sleepy Head.*"

Like a creep, I'd stared at her for five minutes before I said anything. Mel looked beautiful on any given day, but she was at her best when she woke up from a deep sleep. It was about six-thirty in the morning and we'd pretty much slept the night away. After another round of her tryna figure out how much of my dick she could take, I figured I should let the woman rest.

"What time is it?" She grumbled, rolling over to face me with sleepiness in her eyes, plump, chocolate breasts falling from under the covers, hair wild as hell giving me flashbacks of how hard I'd pulled it.

"It's early. Get up and come with me." I said, tugging the covers off the rest of her body, holding out a bright yellow one-piece swimsuit that I'd bought and couldn't wait to see her in.

"Swimming, Olli? Really?" She grunted, trying and failing to snatch the sheets from the foot of the bed before I grabbed them and flung them out of her reach.

I could hardly peel my eyes off her behind. Couldn't believe I was staring at it after pretending it didn't exist for all those years. Mel needed to get her ass out of bed before I wound up back between her legs. I had plans that would expire in the next thirty minutes. And she didn't know it, but I'd cancel them to sit her pussy on my face.

"Don't make me snatch you out this bed." I walked around to the side of the bed, leaning in to pull her hand up and kiss it. "Come on, you gon' miss it."

"Miss what?"

"The sunrise."

"Olli—"

"I *know*, it's corny." I cut her off, grinning because all of this shit was different from what we were used to. "You make me wanna do corny shit. Now, get up before it wears off."

"Okay!" She smiled big, pulling at my arm until I bent down to kiss her lips. Then she hopped out of bed and hurried to the restroom, naked ass jiggling everywhere.

The pool at the back of the lower deck was perfect, and one of the reasons I'd chosen this yacht over all the others. The black owners and black staff were another added bonus. Since we'd be out to sea for a day, we couldn't risk eating unseasoned food.

I'd gone out ahead of Mel and relaxed in one of the reclining beach chairs because I knew how much she hated when I hovered while she got ready. And I was glad that I did. Seeing her approaching me from the other end of the pool was a sight to take in. Wide hips swaying, swimsuit wedged in her ass, fat pussy hidden beneath the too-tight fabric just begging me to kiss it, lick it, suck it.

"Where the hell did you find this 3T bathing suit?" She stopped at the foot of the pool and propped a hand on her hip, having no idea how hard she was making my dick.

"Girl, you finer than a motha fucka!" I sat straight up. "Get your ass over here before Bertrand pulls out his binoculars." I laughed, but I was dead serious.

"I'm coming as fast as I can with this onesie wedged in my behind." She griped. Still didn't stop me from staring, though.

"This is the whitest shit I've ever seen." She teased, hair blowing in the breeze, footing down the blonde wood deck floors, so comfortable in her skin it multiplied her sex appeal by a million.

"Ain't nothin' white about the way you wearin' that bathing suit." I grinned, dick twitching in my shorts.

"Not the *onesie*, nasty ass. All this water." She looked out over the deck.

"Niggas like water too." I chuckled, leaning back against the chair, hands tucked behind my head.

"Says the nigga who avoided the pool at the Y because he swam like a rock and was too scared to get lessons?" She smirked, stopping in front of me, leaving nothing to be imagined about how fat that pussy was.

"I was a lil boy." I looked up at her, pretty ass lips making me wanna stand up and kiss her. "Now I'm a man."

"Shole is." She grinned that sexy ass grin, easing down into the chair to sit between my open legs, ass pushing into my dick as she laid against my chest.

"Can't believe it took me two decades to find out what ole Olli was working with." Now she was playing, wiggling her behind and straining her neck to look back and up at me.

"You wasn't ready." I smiled, staring down into her eyes.

"Still ain't, apparently!" She busted out laughing, and I did too.

"We got time for that." I roped my arms around her waist, leaning in to suck her tongue from her mouth, kissing her deep and long before I remembered what we were out there for.

"Look." I lifted a hand from her belly and pointed out into the water at a perfect view of the horizon just past the railing of the yacht. Roping my arms around her tighter, I leaned in and kissed her neck, breathing in the sweet smell of her body wash. I was intoxicated with all things Melody and couldn't see myself getting enough.

The top of a round orange sphere started rising from behind the water. The slow ascension, similar to the one growing in my shorts, had me feeling all bubbly and floaty and shit. Mel's eyes were fixed on it and her breathing became hurried. I could feel her body reacting to one of nature's simplest gifts. She took a deep breath in and relaxed her head against my chest, reaching her arms up and roping them around the back of my neck as I continued to kiss hers.

"I love you, Olli." She whispered out of nowhere, sending chills up my spine.

"How much?" I asked, sucking her neck hard then soothing it slowly with the spread of my tongue.

"So much." She exhaled, rubbing her fingers down the back of my neck.

My dick jumped against her back and I couldn't control myself any longer, trailing my palms up her belly until they arrived at her breasts. Cupping them and squeezing them and twisting her tight nipples between my fingers, I dragged my teeth along her skin, stopping to suck when that wasn't enough.

"Where's the crew?" She asked, allowing my hands to travel down between her legs.

"Up top." My fingers drifted under the crotch of her swimsuit, tickling her clit and watching her shutter in response.

"We're good," I reassured her, knowing this PDA probably had her on edge. "They ain't comin' down unless I call 'em." I sucked her earlobe, holding her suit to the side and edging my thumb down the spread of her labia before sinking my fingers in.

"I wanna fuck you so bad right now," I whispered in her ear, breath bathing her shoulder as I leaned forward to watch my finger go in and out of her pussy.

"Baby!" She arched her back, closing her thighs around my wrist. Rolling her ass against my dick, she had me hard as a fucking rock.

I forced her knees apart, needing to hear those wet noises coming from between her legs. Turned on by her moaning over the waves crashing against the boat, I unclasped the button holding the crotch of her bathing suit closed and pulled her up on top of me.

Melody pulled her hands from around my neck and braced them on either side of the chair, offering the second it took to flip my dick out over my shorts, before I eased her down over me, toes curling, eyes falling shut. She didn't tense up when the tip slid in, trusting me as I grabbed her hips, temporarily blinded by how good it felt to plunge inside her. She sat up straight, planting her feet on either side of my thighs holding her legs wide open as she slid up and down my length, squeezing me so tight I could feel her pulse through her pussy.

"Olli?"

"Huh?"

"You feel *so* fucking good." She almost cried. Gripping me, and tugging me, and blowing my fucking mind.

Our bodies were in sync, grinding against each other, damp with sweat and the need to be connected forever in this way. I felt helpless. Like nothing else mattered and no one else would do. The picture of perfection was her bending forward, bracing her palms on my thighs, ass bouncing before me with the bottom of her swimsuit rolled up around her waist. Deeper and longer and harder I stroked, dying to release, painfully swelling against her walls.

She circled her hips in perfect rhythm, massaging my dick in slow motion. Had me firing off at all cylinders at the sound of her moaning and telling me how good the dick felt, and how the pussy was mine, and how she'd fuck me anytime and anyplace and couldn't wait to feel my cum shooting deep, deep inside her. Hearing the breathlessness in her voice, I leaned her back against my chest, and hooked my arms under her knees, spreading her wide open and letting the breeze kiss her openness. Aching with the desire to be covered in her love, I anchored myself, abandoning all thoughts of being anywhere but right there between those chocolate legs. The inside of Melody was a blissful place. She had me dizzy, and manic, and completely fucking sprung.

A heaviness pooled in the pit of my stomach. The need to release was as necessary as breathing. "Fuck!" She screamed with her eyes blinking closed. "Make me cum!" She begged, surrendering to the stroke.

The harder I fucked her the louder she screamed, wet noises from her center pushing me closer to the edge. The softness of her skin rubbed up and down my chest, leaving little to no resistance inside of me.

"God!" I held her legs open as wide as they'd go.

"Melody." My voice was weak and so were my knees.

"Baby." I breathed out, lips trailing the side of her neck.

"I fuckin' love you." I trembled in response to her contracting around me, meeting her there at the peak as we surrendered to it all.

Melody

Beneath the warmth of the sun, we lie there on the deck, wrapped in each other's arms forgetting the rest of the world. Though barely clothed, I felt covered by something that I'd known for a long time, but never in this way. Olli's lips trailed up and down my neck, stopping to suckle my skin as if he, like me, couldn't believe this was real. And then he spoke words that I'd heard him say before. Only this time, I knew that they were coming from a completely different place.

"I really do love you." His voice, like bass, vibrated against the sensitive skin on my neck, sending ripples of his energy trailing down to the tips of my toes and out through the points of my fingertips and nipples. Still submerged inside me, it felt like we were one. No more hiding from what was real. No pretending not to feel. Just living inside a love that had yet to be defined. A love that was his. A love that was mine. Neither of us had been searching for what we'd found. But there we were, in love.

The end...

MORE STORIES BY SABRINA

LENA

YOURS TRULY… OR SOMETHING LIKE THAT (BOOK ONE)

YOURS TRULY… LOST AND FOUND (BOOK TWO)

BODIES: SECRETS, FLESH, & BLOOD (BOOK ONE)

BODIES: BLACK & BLUE (BOOK TWO)

BODIES: CARRIED AWAY (BOOK THREE)

STONE BODIES PRODUCTIONS: THE GRIND (BOOK ONE)

STONE BODIES PRODUCTIONS: THE FALL (BOOK TWO)

NO LOVE (A STORY OF LOVE AVOIDED)

THE LAKE (A NOVELETTE)

BUTTERFLIES IN A MASON JAR

SO, THIS IS CHRISTMAS? (A NOVEL)

SHAW SIBLINGS AFTER-WORDS: KEYS AND CHORUSES-JORDYN & RUSSELL (BOOK ONE)

SHAW SIBLINGS AFTER-WORDS: ADDICTED-JESSIE & CHLOE (BOOK TWO)

SHAW SIBLINGS AFTER-WORDS: SEPARATED-JOSH & SIMONE (BOOK THREE)

A SCATTERED LIFE SERIES: SIX MARBLE HEADSTONES (BOOK ONE)

THE BRICKS: APT. B17 CAMILLE (BOOK ONE)

THE BRICKS: APT. F53 TASIA (BOOK TWO)

THE BRICKS: APT. F58 KESHIA (BOOK THREE)

THE BRICKS: APT. A1 FREDDIE (BOOK FOUR)

A COLLECTION OF CHRISTMAS STORIES FROM THE BRICKS

PETALS

THE COLOR SPECTRUM DUET: IVORY (BOOK ONE)

THE COLOR SPECTRUM: EBONY (BOOK TWO) BY CHENCIA C. HIGGINS

HOW TO LOVE

WHO TO LOVE

NAUGHTY: AN EROTIC CHRISTMAS NOVELLA

NASTY (AN EROTIC SPIN-OFF)

PLUS

THE FOLD THOU SHALL NOT RUN (BOOK ONE)
THOU SHALL NOT HIDE (BOOK TWO)
DESDEMONA'S CLOSET

TO THE READERS…
THANK YOU SO MUCH FOR TAKING THE TIME TO
READ THIS STORY.
I HOPE YOU ENJOYED READING IT AS MUCH AS I
ENJOYED WRITING IT!
FOR MORE OF MY STORIES, PLEASE VISIT MY
AUTHOR PAGE
ON AMAZON.COM @ SABRINA B. SCALES.
AND PLEASE, RATE AND REVIEW.
IT'S THE BEST GIFT ANY READER CAN LEAVE FOR AN
AUTHOR,
WORTH MORE THAN ITS WEIGHT IN GOLD!
FOR INQUIRIES, PLEASE CONTACT ME AT:
SABRINABSCALES@GMAIL.COM
OR
ON FACEBOOK AUTHOR SABRINA B. SCALES
OR
ON INSTAGRAM @AUHTORSABRINABSCALES
THANKS A BUNCH. KEEP READING!